STONE

IRON ROGUES MC

FIONA DAVENPORT

STONE

Britta Hughes was too young and innocent for Shaw "Stone" Jackson when they first met, so he had to wait to claim her. On the run for her life, his club president helped her disappear. Not knowing her location drove the Iron Rogues Captain up the wall, but he lived with it because Britta's safety came first.

Even though she'd only known Stone for a few days before she left, Britta never forgot him. So when her mom disappeared, she ran straight to the biker who'd starred in her dreams for the past two years.

PROLOGUE
BRITTA

"We're gonna have to get you out of the city to keep you safe. Tommaso isn't going to let you go unless it's in a casket." My best friend's dad shifted his attention from my mom toward me. "And he'll send your daughter with you because he's a vengeful prick."

I didn't have big plans, but sitting by my mom's bedside in the hospital was not how I wanted to spend my birthday. Most girls at my school dreamed about spending their sweet sixteen at a huge party where they were the center of everyone's attention. Not me, though.

The thought of a bunch of people staring at me all night long gave me the heebie-jeebies. I had learned years ago that it was smarter to fade into the background. And I knew better than to hope for something that would never happen since my mom couldn't afford to spoil me like that on what she earned as a bartender.

Considering the situation my mom had gotten us in, I would've gladly had every person from my school at a party where I stood naked on a stage while they stared at me all night long. Anything would've been better than my mom being beaten almost to death by her boyfriend.

"Whatever you think is best," I replied before my mom could say anything. I didn't trust her to make the right decision, especially when it had anything to do with one of her boyfriends.

My mom had the worst taste in men. My dad had bailed on her when she turned up pregnant with me, and each of the guys she got with since as far back as I could remember somehow managed to be worse than the one before. Her most recent boyfriend was awful enough that I'd been thinking about running away from home for the past few days.

I'd thought something was off about Tommaso the first time she'd introduced me to him, but Mom tended to see the best in the guys she dated. He was attractive, dressed well, drove a nice car, and took her out on nice dates...and that was good enough for her.

But his son made me really uncomfortable. He was four years older than me and watched me with too much interest. It gave me the creeps.

I wanted to kick myself for not noticing that he'd been hurting her. When she'd been admitted to the hospital a couple of months ago, she'd lied to me about her "accident." There had been no car that had hit her, just Tommaso's fists. And it wasn't the last time.

After she was discharged, he kept the hits away from her face so that nobody would ask any questions, and she always had a handy excuse for why she was moving slower than usual. A twisted ankle because she was hurrying into work so she wouldn't be late for her shift. A pulled muscle from lifting a keg when nobody else was around to help out during a busy Friday night. A strained back because she was getting up in years.

It wasn't until I got the call that she was back in the hospital again that I learned she'd been hiding what he'd been doing to her. She hadn't told me, even then. I'd overheard a couple of nurses whispering about how her injuries didn't match up to the story she'd told and that they should probably call the police.

When I confronted my mom about it, she

freaked out. I hadn't understood why she didn't want the cops involved. Why she wouldn't dump Tommaso, no matter how much I begged her. All she'd said was that leaving him wasn't possible and the police couldn't help her.

I was only sixteen and had nowhere else to go, but the thought of spending the next two years watching my mom get beaten up by the guy who should've kissed the ground she walked on was almost more than I could bear.

With nobody else to go to, I called my best friend. Izzy's dad was a biker and belonged to a motorcycle club. Rubble was sweet with me and Izzy, but he was also a big, intimidating man, and I had this wild idea that maybe he could warn Tommaso off so he'd leave my mom alone. An hour after my call, he showed up in my mom's hospital room with three other guys who looked just as scary. He explained that he could get us safely away from Tommaso. Only then did my mom confess to everything that had been going on.

Tommaso wasn't just an abusive boyfriend. He was the enforcer for a local crime boss. A group involved in smuggling drugs and…people.

Rubble moved quickly, sending one of the other bikers to grab our vital necessities before coming back to pick us up. The next thing I knew, he was sneaking my mom out of her room and down to a car idling at the curb in front of the emergency room entrance.

When we were safely in the back seat, he crouched low to stare into my eyes. "You're not gonna be able to talk to Izzy again anytime soon, but I'll let her know you're safe. You can trust the guys I'm sending you to. They'll look out for you and your mom."

"Thank you."

He dipped his chin to acknowledge my gratitude before slamming the door shut and pounding his fist against the roof of the car.

The driver peeled away, and Mom reached over to pat my thigh. "I'm so sorry I got you into this mess, sweetie."

Staring out the passenger window into the darkness, I whispered, "It's okay."

It really wasn't, but with one of her eyes almost swollen shut and the other bruises I'd caught a glimpse of when she'd been changing, I couldn't bring myself to yell at her. She knew as well as I did that her choices had put us in danger. Pitching a fit, no matter how well deserved, wouldn't do any good.

"It's not." She cast a furtive glance at the guy

driving us away from the town I'd grown up in. "But I swear to you that I'll do whatever it takes to make sure you're safe."

The eight-hour drive to the tiny town of Old Bridge, Tennessee, wasn't how I'd expected to spend my birthday, but I had nothing to complain about. After that long ride, I got the best birthday gifts I could've hoped for—freedom from Tommaso and meeting the man of my dreams.

Several members of the Iron Rogues chapter Izzy's dad had sent us to were waiting up for us, but I only had eyes for one of them. Stone was tall and muscular, with dark brown hair and bright blue eyes. He was closer in age to my mom than me, but that didn't stop me from falling for him at first sight. Or knowing that I was going to miss him so much when the president of his chapter decided we would be safer somewhere else. Even though he kept his distance from me during the few days we were in Tennessee, I could see the same spark in his eyes when he looked at me. Deep down in my soul, I knew this was more than a schoolgirl crush. We were meant to be together. I just hoped he felt the same way.

1

STONE

I wasn't asleep when my alarm went off, but seeing as I was already in a shit mood, I grabbed it and threw it at the wall, smashing it to pieces.

I'd been thinking about this day for two fucking years and had done everything I could to prepare for it. But nothing had worked out the way I'd planned.

It was her birthday.

She was eighteen.

Finally, I could make her mine.

Except the shit that took her away from me hadn't been resolved.

Britta Hughes had been barely sixteen when she and her mother came to the Iron Rogues for help.

Motorcycle Clubs were secretive by nature, but there were a few things the public knew. No one

could say that we lived on the right side of the law...
we had blood on our hands, dealt in shady shit, and
had our own brand of justice. But we also had honor,
loyalty, and limits. We even worked with the local
law enforcement from time to time—outside of Old
Bridge, because we basically owned the small town
and our own laws were the only ones enforced there.

When it came to certain things, we were the
judge, jury, and even executioner. We didn't tolerate
drugs anywhere near our territory, and human traf-
fickers had a habit of disappearing when brought to
our attention.

But in the right circles, people also knew we
would protect those who needed it. They knew they
could come to us for help, even in the event that they
needed to disappear. Unlike the government who
tossed people into WITSEC—and attempted to
handle the problem legally—we simply eliminated
the fucking threat.

Britta's mother, Marylin, had been unknowingly
working as a bartender for one of the biggest crime
bosses in Chicago, and she also happened to be in a
relationship with one of his enforcers. She
confronted him when she overheard him talking to
an associate about a shipment of girls.

He beat the shit out of her and told her to keep

her mouth shut. Then he threatened Britta to keep Marylin in the relationship.

He'd never touched her in anger before that incident, but he must have gotten a taste for it because the beatings continued, the frequency and intensity increasing.

We had an Iron Rogues chapter just north of the city. One of the officers had a daughter who went to school with Britta. They had become good friends, and the next time Marylin ended up in the hospital, the girl went to her dad.

He contacted Fox, who agreed to help the mother and daughter hide until we could handle the issue and allow them to come out of hiding.

When they arrived at our clubhouse, I'd taken one look at Britta with her wavy blond hair, jade-green eyes, and incredible curves and knew she would be mine someday. But despite the fact that she had the body of a woman and had clearly been forced to grow up too fucking fast, she was only sixteen.

She was too fucking young for me. Even if she had been legal, there were still fourteen years between us. But that wasn't going to stop me when the time came.

I had to ignore the sparks between us and keep

my distance until she was of age, but that didn't mean I wouldn't watch over her. I protected what was mine.

But then the choice was taken away from me.

Fox had made all the arrangements and refused to tell me anything. No matter how many times I petitioned him to give me the details and let me protect her.

Fox didn't want my presence bringing attention to them or risking that Britta would notice me and blow her cover trying to see me.

His decision was logical, but when it came to Britta, I wasn't in a rational frame of mind.

I'd always been a laid-back guy. Quick with a smile and a joke, even though I was torn up and broken inside. An incident in my past had left deep wounds, but I kept them to myself and only let the anger and sorrow out when we were interrogating scum or delivering justice to people who didn't deserve to live.

However, since Fox first denied my request to keep watch over Britta, I'd slowly lost the ability to pretend. The closer I got to her birthday, the fouler my mood was. Every time Fox denied me access to my woman, it got even worse.

Lately, I was basically in a constant state of

asshole. I just didn't have the emotional capacity to give a fuck.

My phone vibrated on the small table next to my bed, and I scowled as I grabbed it. The text was from Fox, telling me we needed to meet about club business in thirty minutes.

I'd lived at the clubhouse the past five years, ever since I'd patched in at twenty-seven. Although, I'd been looking for a new place recently because I wasn't gonna live here with Britta.

I decided to hurry and get ready so I could hopefully have a few minutes with Prez before everyone else arrived.

Fox was reading a document when I entered, but he lowered it to the desk when I approached.

He took one look at my face and shook his head. "No."

"She's eighteen today," I stated, even though I knew he was perfectly aware of what day it was.

Fox's eyes narrowed as he leaned back in his chair. "Doesn't change my answer, Stone."

The warning was clear in his tone, but my fury and desperation blinded me. "Need to know they're safe," I said through gritted teeth.

"I would tell you if they weren't. And like I've

said many times, you'll be my first call when the time is right."

"Who decides when the time is right?" I growled.

Fox leaned forward, and his eyes hardened, the cold depths clearly showing the ruthless leader we all feared and respected. "You questioning my decisions, citizen?"

I swallowed hard and shook my head.

"Thin fucking ice, Stone. Now sit your ass down and wait for the others. We have shit to deal with."

I needed this meeting to be over as soon as fucking possible. Before my rage consumed me, and I did something stupid.

"Need your head in the game, Stone," Fox continued. He handed me a slip of paper with a date, time, and address. "Gonna send Viper with you. You need someone to watch your back."

Translation: I needed someone to make sure I didn't lose focus and muck shit up. *Fair enough.*

I knew he wouldn't tell me anything else until the others arrived, so I took a deep breath and tried to calm down as I ambled over to a couch and dropped down onto it. The paper crumpled as my hands curled into fists, and I rested them on my thighs.

Maverick was grinning smugly when he and

Viper, our tail gunner, walked into the room together. "Molly needed my help with something," he told Viper.

"Guessing it was the same thing Rhiannon needed *help* with," Viper quipped.

"Seriously?" I snapped. "You're late because you were fu—"

"Don't finish that sentence, Stone," Fox interrupted with a scowl. "Unless you want an ass-kicking that would put you in traction for a month."

I pressed my lips together, holding back the caustic remark that was on the tip of my tongue. Crossing my arms over my chest, I leaned back into the couch.

"You're being more of an asshole than usual," Viper observed as he took one of the chairs at a small, round table on the opposite side of Fox's desk.

I frowned intensely at him but remained quiet.

"He's pissed at me," Fox explained, not sounding nearly as angry as I expected.

Viper raised a brow, and Mav huffed as he went around the desk and settled himself against the wall just to the left of the prez. "Britta?" he guessed.

"She's eighteen," I growled.

"And we still haven't eliminated the threat to

them," Mav argued. "As soon as we do and it's safe for them, you'll have their location."

We'd been working on taking out the organization that was targeting Marylin and Britta. It was unusual for us to take this long to get shit handled. However, we had to take down the boss for the girls to be truly safe. His name and location were so closely guarded that our only option had been to start at the bottom of the ladder. No one knew the players in the group who were above their direct supervisor, so we interrogated one and moved up to the next, then did it again. Sometimes multiple people were on the next rung, which meant hunting them all down until we figured out who had the information we needed to continue to climb.

Glaring at Mav, I unfolded my arms, and my hands curled into fists again as I rested them on my knees. "I protect what's mine."

"Enough," Fox barked. "Do not question my orders, Stone. I've let you get away with a lot of shit when it involved Britta because I understand your frustration. But if you take it too far, I'll have your patch. Understood?"

I watched him warily for a moment. He was right. It was rare for the prez or VP to put up with the kind of shit I'd been giving them for the past two years. Clearly, I'd reached their limit. So I nodded and tried to relax.

Fox jerked his chin up and down with finality, then turned to face his computer. "An informant just passed along word of an auction he's heard about. Gave us a time and location, but he wasn't sure how accurate the intel is."

"Fuck," Viper muttered.

"Same motherfuckers?" I asked.

"Looks like it."

We'd been stalking a trafficking ring for a few months, but every time we got close, they were gone —along with the girls—by the time we arrived. With every miss, I got closer to the edge of my rage and sanity. One of the few things that kept me from losing my mind was thinking about what I was gonna do to those fuckers when we finally found them.

"Where did the information come from?" Viper asked. Likely thinking as I was, that our informants had been less than reliable in the past.

"Wouldn't tell me," Fox grunted. "But he was adamant that it was accurate. Never seen him so determined to have me believe him."

"Inside man?" Mav suggested.

Fox shrugged and scrubbed his hands over his face. "No fucking clue. But if we don't take these assholes down this time, heads are gonna roll. I will bring in every informant, every person who ever gave us even the slightest inkling that they knew something or might have been involved. By the time we're done with them, they'll be spilling every fucking secret they have."

Viper nodded in agreement. "Details?"

"New York. In the port district." Fox handed him a slip of paper, and he glanced at it, frowning deeply when he saw the date, time, and address.

"That's over a thirteen-hour drive," I grumbled.

Fox grunted, "Gives me time to touch base with Nic."

Nic DeLuca was the head of the New York Mafia and a client of the Iron Rogues. But he was also a close friend of Fox's. "His organization has been after the same group, so I asked him to do more digging into the accuracy of the tip. And no one will know you two."

I tuned out whatever the three of them said next, but my attention was snagged when something flew through the air, and Viper caught it.

Jealousy burned in my gut when he held up a property vest. He was headed home to give it to his woman.

There was a similar vest hanging in my closet.

Only this one said, "Property of Stone." Fox had given it to me shortly after the first time he refused to tell me where my girl was.

"It's gonna happen," he'd told me. "Now you'll be ready when it does."

———

It took over a week to resolve the situation in New York. We'd teamed up with the DeLucas and managed to bust the operation in time to save the latest shipment of girls.

Before we left, we had dinner with Nic, his wife Anna, and their cute kids. Afterward, Nic asked me to join him in his home office.

He walked around his large, mahogany desk and sat down. "Have a seat," he offered, gesturing to the leather wingback chairs in front of him.

I watched him tap on a laptop as I sat.

After a minute, he wrote something on a slip of paper and handed it to me.

"The head of the family in Chicago"—and by family, he meant the Mafia—"is a good friend. Kye explained your situation to me, and I reached out to Francesco to see if he could be of any help."

I glanced at the paper and saw the name Francesco Bianchi and a phone number.

"He offered to assist in any way he could. He was already familiar with the organization that you're trying to take down. They knew about the drugs and prostitution rings but not that the girls were being bought and sold. Like me, Francesco does not tolerate human trafficking. As you've discovered, they are not easy to infiltrate, and taking them down one by one is a long-drawn-out process. He has some ideas on how to move forward that I think could be very valuable."

Nic gestured to the paper. "He's expecting your call."

"Mine?" I raised a brow, and Nic cocked his head as he studied me. "Kye said you were in charge of the operation to nail these *figli di puttana*. Was I misinformed?"

"No," I replied. I was gonna fucking owe my prez big for giving this to me. Especially when I'd been such a bastard lately.

"Thanks," I said with an appreciative nod as I stood. We shook hands, and he inclined his head. "*Buona fortuna*," he said, wishing us luck.

2

BRITTA

The past two years had been pretty good to me. My mom and I were safe in the small town where we'd settled. Money wasn't as tight as it'd been growing up since she was working in a bar owned by the Hounds of Hellfire, a club with which the Iron Rogues apparently had a loose connection. I'd been so far ahead in schoolwork when transferring that I was able to graduate a semester early last month. And my mom had stayed away from men, which had done wonders for our relationship.

The only thing missing from my life was Stone.

None of the boys I'd met in school had caught my interest the way he had. They all seemed so... young in comparison. Which made sense when you considered they were only teenagers and he was in his thirties. But weirdly, I felt as though there was more of a gap between those boys and me than what I had with Stone.

My childhood had left a mark on me, and I felt older than the eighteen years I'd celebrated with my mom a few months ago. Being abandoned by your father, your mom getting hospitalized by her abusive boyfriend more than once, and running for your life tended to do that to a person. So did being mostly on your own.

Since I had serious trust issues from my dad, I'd always had a hard time making friends. Everything that had happened with Tommaso had sent my walls higher, so I hadn't made any close ones since we left Chicago. And I wasn't allowed to talk to Izzy because it wasn't safe for her or me. We had to go to those lengths so my mom and I couldn't be traced. Cutting off contact with everyone we knew from our previous lives.

These were deep thoughts for the grocery store, so I shook them off and headed toward the checkout area. I flashed the cashier a half smile as she scanned my items.

"Having a good day?" she asked.

I nodded. "Yup."

"You've lived here a couple of years now, right?"

I pressed my lips together to hold back an irritated sigh. "Mm-hmm."

Her gaze darted around to make sure nobody else was nearby before she leaned forward. "I could swear I've seen you talking to a few different members of the Hounds of Hellfire. Are you a club girl or something?"

I'd learned as much as I could about club life since we came here—figuring that it would help if my dream of being with Stone ever came true—but I had no idea what she was talking about. "Am I a what?"

"You know...a club whore or whatever the Hounds of Hellfire like to call the women who are there for them to sleep with whenever they want."

My head jerked back, my eyes going wide. "Absolutely not."

Her gaze raked down what she could see of my body and back up again, her lips curving into a smirk. "Yeah, now that I think about it, that's kind of a ridiculous question. You look way too innocent to be banging a bunch of bikers, most of whom are twice your age."

With the Iron Rogues and Hounds of Hellfire looking out for my mom and me, I'd spent a few days each at a couple of different clubhouses. Not once had I ever seen anything like this woman was describing. But I didn't bother correcting her or defending my looks since she wasn't worth the effort —and I would never betray a club secret, no matter how small or unimportant. Not when they'd done so much for us. Or with my feelings for Stone.

Instead, I just murmured, "You almost done?"

She pursed her lips and nodded, picking up the pace as she finished checking me out. I helped her bag my stuff, and then I loaded everything into the car that the Hounds of Hellfire president had gotten for us before we moved into the apartment. I drove straight home and hurried inside.

"I'm home," I called, kicking the door shut behind me before heading toward the kitchen to drop the bags on the counter. "And you won't believe what happened while I was at the store. They definitely need better customer service training with the way the cashier who helped me talks to shoppers."

There was no answer, and I assumed my mom had fallen asleep in her bedroom. Working nights wreaked havoc on her schedule, and she squeezed in extra sleep whenever she could. So after putting away the groceries, I tiptoed down the hallway until I noticed her door was open. "Mom?"

Finding her bed a wreck and the lamp on the floor, I gasped. "No. No. No."

I searched the apartment, but she was gone. And now that I was paying closer attention, I noticed little things that I had missed when I first got back. Her winter coat was on the floor beneath the hooks we used to hang them by the door. The end table next to the couch had been pushed forward about a foot, and the book she'd been reading last night was on the floor in front of it.

Her purse still hung on its hook, and I had our car. So there was only one explanation that made sense...someone had taken my mom.

I hadn't seen or heard from Stone in all that time, but he was the first person I thought of. There were a couple of Hounds of Hellfire prospects who lived in the same building, but I didn't even stop to consider going to one of them. Or the Hounds of Hellfire clubhouse.

Instead, I ran into my room and packed a few changes of clothes and my toiletries. Then I dug through my mom's purse for the cash from her tips last night. Only I found more than I was looking for and not in a good way.

There were four threatening notes shoved all the way at the bottom. They all had the same theme— keep your mouth shut if you want to live. The last one I read scared me the most.

Whores like you can't be trusted. Such a shame that your daughter will have to pay for your mistakes.

I was being threatened, but she hadn't said a word to me about the notes. And my guess was that she hadn't told the Hounds of Hellfire either. At the very least, they would have wanted to help track down whoever sent them. More likely, they would've moved us again.

I didn't know what she'd been thinking, and the only way I'd ever find out was if I got her back. I needed help for that, so I turned the three-hour drive to Old Bridge into a little over two as I broke every speed limit.

A prospect was manning the entrance to the compound. His eyes went wide when I stopped within an inch of the gate. Rolling down my window, I didn't give him the chance to say anything before I demanded, "Get Stone. Now!"

"Who do you think you are to tell me what—"

Undoing my seat belt, I flung my car door open and jumped out. "I'm under Iron Rogues protection. If you turn me away, you'll never get patched in."

"Fuck," he muttered, eyeing me speculatively. Then he pulled out his cell and stabbed his finger against the screen. It wasn't long before someone picked up, and he growled, "Need you to come out to the gate. A girl here says she's under our protection and needs help. She's asking for you."

A few minutes later, the gate opened, and the prospect waved me through. As I approached the clubhouse, the man I'd been dreaming of for two long years stalked out. I was back with Stone. Finally.

3

STONE

"Talked to Francesco last night," I informed Maverick as I pushed a glass of whiskey toward him.

I'd been pouring one for myself when he entered the lounge and came to sit at the bar.

Since we were alone, it was safe to discuss club business outside his office.

When I returned from New York, Fox had given me permission to make taking out the threat to Britta my number one priority. I'd been working day and night for three months to handle this shit.

Finally, we were making some headway.

"His man finally get in the right circle?" Mav asked.

I nodded before tipping my glass back and swallowing half the contents.

"The family staged it to look like Carlos took out Francesco's number two, including his wife and kids. Darius"—who we'd discovered was working directly for the crime boss's head of security—"took it as a sign of loyalty and introduced him to...get this..." I emptied my glass before dropping my bomb on Mav. "Portia."

Maverick spit out the sip of whiskey he'd just taken and stared at me in complete shock. "No fucking way."

"I couldn't make this shit up, brother. The head of security is a fucking woman."

Before Mav could respond, my cell phone rang. It was on the bar top to my left, so I glanced at the screen, fully intending to ignore it.

However, it was the number from the security booth at the gate. "It's Jimmy," I said with a frown as I picked up my phone.

"Is there a problem?" Mav asked, pulling out his phone to open the security feed from the cameras out front.

I shrugged and answered, putting it on speaker. "Stone."

"Need you to come out to the gate. A girl here says she's under our protection and needs help. She's asking for you."

"Son of a bitch," Maverick cursed. "Fox is gonna lose his fucking mind."

Before I could ask, he showed me the screen, and everything in me froze.

"Let her through," Mav grunted to Jimmy since I was obviously incapable of thinking about anything except the woman with the curvy body and gorgeous blond hair.

Reality returned in a rush, and I slammed my glass on the bar top so hard it cracked. "He's not going to keep her from me," I seethed, feeling homicidal at the thought of losing Britta again.

"I'll handle it. Go."

I stalked around the bar and across the room, then into the hallway, yanking the door open so hard it crashed into the wall.

The car I'd seen on the camera was just pulling up as I exited the clubhouse, and I headed straight for it.

I was nearly there when the door swung open, and Britta came flying out, her long hair streaming behind her as she ran straight into my arms.

Holy fuck. I'd waited so long to feel her body pressed against mine. My dreams couldn't hold a candle to the real thing.

The thought that there must be something wrong if she was here hung on the periphery of my mind, but I was too consumed with my desperate need for her to consider anything rational right then.

I closed my arms around her, holding her plastered against me, but I glided one hand up her back and tangled it in her hair. Firmly but gently, I pulled on it until her face was tilted up.

Then I crashed my mouth down on hers.

Britta melted against me immediately, and I grunted in approval as I held her even tighter.

She let out a little gasp, and I plunged my tongue inside to taste her sweetness.

My need for her was primal, and the kiss quickly became carnal. It was only the chill of the late January wind that reminded me where we were before I lost my mind and fucked her right there on the grass in front of the clubhouse.

But it was only the reminder that she was probably in danger that gave me enough strength to end my assault on her mouth.

"Stone," she sighed, relief evident in her tone as

she rested her cheek against my chest. "I need your help."

"Shaw," I corrected.

"What?" she asked, looking up at me, her expression confused.

"Stone is my road name, baby. You call me Shaw."

"Oh." Her cheeks turned adorably pink, and her lips curled up into a pretty smile, but it dropped half a second later as her expression darkened with fear.

I was about to ask about it, but she shivered, and I realized she was only wearing a sweater. Tennessee generally had mild weather, but January was still our coldest month, and it was in the low fifties.

"Let's get you inside. Then we can talk," I muttered as I released her, although I kept one arm around her as I led her to the front door.

Maverick was waiting just inside, and he nodded at her in greeting. "Britta. I'd say nice to see you, but I assume you wouldn't be here unless there was a problem."

He turned and led the way down the hall in the opposite direction of the lounge.

"Where are we going?" she asked softly, looking around with apprehension.

"Maverick's office. So we can talk in privacy, baby. You have nothing to worry about."

"Fox is on his way," Mav said over his shoulder as he strolled through the door to a room that looked similar to the prez's office. However, the decor made it obvious who belonged in each one.

Britta frowned. "Will he be here soon? Because I need help fast."

He gave me a look and added, "He was...at The Room."

I nodded in acknowledgment. The Room was a small, nondescript building on the back of the fenced property. We used it to deal with...people who needed encouragement to talk or ones who needed to be put in the ground.

"He'll only be a couple of minutes, baby."

"Have a seat," Maverick suggested. Once he sat behind his desk and I had settled Britta on the couch next to me, Mav smiled at her. He had a way of putting people at ease, something we'd had in common until Britta was ripped away from me and I grew into an angry bastard all the time.

Maverick's expression was soft when he asked Britta, "Texted a few other enforcers to join us, just so everyone has the details firsthand. Are you comfortable with that?"

She looked up at me, and I smiled before kissing her forehead. Returning her gaze to Mav, her voice was strong when she agreed. "Yes. But will they be long? My mom—"

She was cut off by a "Yo" as Deviant—an enforcer and our resident tech genius—strolled through the door. He dropped into a chair next to a medium-sized conference table on the opposite side of the room from Britta and me. He observed us for a second, then his brow rose in question.

"Britta came to us for help," I explained.

Fox stalked into the room before I could say anything else.

His expression was fierce, but he smoothed it over when he looked at Britta. He glanced at me, then at Britta's other side, probably looking for her mom. When his eyes came back to me, they were furious.

"She came to us, Prez," Maverick explained, probably assuming where Fox's mind had gone.

His scowl eased up, and he turned his attention back to my girl. "Where's Marylin?"

"That's why I came—"

"Hold up, Britta," Mav interjected, his eyes directed at the door to his office.

Whiskey—our sergeant at arms—and two other

enforcers, Racer and Hunter, walked in and joined Deviant at the table.

Fox braced his feet apart and crossed his arms over his chest in an intimidating stance. However, he softened it by smiling encouragingly at Britta. "What's going on, B?"

I scowled at his use of a nickname for my woman but now wasn't the time to address it. Especially not when she described what she found at her apartment only a few hours ago.

Fox's face twisted with rage, and I had a feeling I knew why. The fury was burning in my gut, and if Britta hadn't been there, I'd have been swearing up a blue streak and putting my fist through a wall.

Fox pivoted to face the table where the other guys sat. "Deviant, focus on finding Marylin."

"Why don't I put Grey on Marilyn so I can focus on the...other thing?"

Fox nodded. "Marylin is the priority, so if Grey isn't available—"

"On it," Deviant replied, already out of his seat and headed for the door.

I felt Britta's relief in her posture as she watched him leave. She didn't know many of us, but she knew Deviant's role since he'd been integral to her relocation.

Prez was still barking orders to the other when Britta whispered, "Who is Grey?"

"A tech genius who belongs to the Silver Saints MC. Fox's and Maverick's old ladies are the president's daughters, so we have a close alliance with them."

Everyone but Maverick left the office, and Fox turned his attention back to me and Britta. "Get B settled in your room. Gonna have a talk with King," —King was the road name for Connor Kingsley, who had taken over as president of the Hounds of Hellfire when the last guy retired—"and we'll meet in your office in half an hour."

Letting the nickname thing go again...for now, I nodded and climbed to my feet before holding out my hand to help Britta up.

"I'll send Molly to you just before the meeting," Maverick offered. "She can take her to get something to eat and show her around a little."

"Thank you," Britta answered as I led her toward the door.

We walked toward the back of the building, where several rooms belonged to members or were empty for anyone who needed to crash at the clubhouse.

The entire second floor was also rooms, but I'd

chosen one on the ground floor. It wasn't far from my office, which was convenient when I needed to work late. Something that happened more than I liked since I was the club's lawyer.

With the number of clients our various club-owned businesses had, I was often bogged down by contracts. Then there was the legal shit involved in keeping my brothers out of jail or defending them if needed. And a staggering amount of paperwork came with owning the majority of a town.

Unlike a lot of clubs, the Iron Rogues had a very small compound that only had the clubhouse, some wooded areas, and The Room. It was hidden on the outskirts of town. Rather than building a fortress, we owned 90 percent of the land and businesses in Old Bridge. Anyone who lived within the town limits was a member, family member, or basically had to be approved by the MC.

Owning all the businesses and rental properties was enough to keep me busy, but I also handled the legal side of selling empty houses or lots to patched members who didn't want to live in the clubhouse. That had become much more frequent since so many of my brothers had claimed old ladies and started families.

"My office," I murmured to Britta, pointing at a

closed door. Britta had a lot to learn about life in an MC, so I figured I might as well start right away.

We reached my room, and I unlocked it before ushering her inside. Then I pulled her into my arms and stared down at her. "You're my priority, baby. Always. You need anything, you come to me. Don't ever feel like you're interrupting or unwelcome."

Britta smiled warmly, her beautiful green eyes nearly making me forget what I'd been about to say.

"But there will be shit that I'm not allowed to share with you. Sometimes I'll come out to talk to you rather than letting you in."

She nodded, and I was relieved when her expression held acceptance rather than anger.

"In private, you can argue with me, yell, throw things, whatever. Even around my brothers, to a certain extent. But in front of prospects or other visitors, we have to keep up appearances, so you'll have to do as I say without question."

She stared at me thoughtfully for a second, then her expression turned cheeky and she asked, "But when we're alone, I can scream at you?"

I laughed and brushed a kiss over her mouth before whispering in her ear, "Baby, you'll definitely be screaming when we're alone. For a whole different reason."

Britta's face turned pink, and a little smile lifted the corners of her mouth.

Just as quickly, her smile disappeared, and her green pools darkened. She sighed and hugged me tight, casting her eyes down before resting her cheek against my chest.

4

BRITTA

I hated that my mom was missing, but I was finally with Shaw after two long years. I felt guilty over how happy I was to be in his arms when I didn't even know if she was still alive. Sniffling, I pressed my face against his broad chest.

"What's wrong, baby?" he asked, pressing a finger under my chin to tilt my head back, his gorgeous blue eyes filled with concern.

"I'm warm and protected in your arms—where I've dreamed of being for the past two years—but my mom is out there. Someone could be hurting her right now. Or worse," I rasped, tears streaming down my cheeks.

"I get where you're coming from, but there will be no regrets when it comes to you and me being together, Britta." He stroked his thumb across my cheek. "And you gotta know that I'll do everything in my power to make sure your mom comes home to you."

"Just so long as nothing bad happens to you while you're doing it," I whispered.

"You don't need to worry about me, baby. Good old Uncle Sam trained me well, and five years as an Iron Rogue has only honed those skills."

His reassurances helped soothe some of my nerves as I looked around his room, surprised by how clean it was. The one I had shared with my mom when we'd been here two years ago had been nice enough, but I had assumed that the rooms the men used would be more...lived in. Or downright dirty based on how my mom's boyfriends never seemed to know how to clean.

Wanting to help where I could after all he'd done for me, I offered, "I can take over for your cleaner if you'd like."

"Cleaner?" he echoed, his brows drawing together.

I swept my arm in a half circle to gesture around the room. "Whoever keeps your room like this. Your bed is made so well, I bet I could bounce a quarter off your mattress."

He shook his head with a laugh that sent a shiver of awareness down my spine. "That'd be me, baby. Another thing being in the military taught me."

"Oh." I giggled, and his eyes darkened a shade.

Tugging me toward the bed, he suggested, "Maybe we should test your theory, but with something different than a quarter."

I eyed the mattress, my panties growing damp. "Um...didn't Maverick say that he was going to send Molly for me?"

"Fuck." Shaw sighed and raked his fingers through his hair. "You make it too damn easy to forget everything else."

I felt a feminine thrill at knowing I could distract this man. He was so confident and sexy, but I was able to throw him off course. Knowing the impact I had on him gave me the courage to go after what I wanted. Rolling up on my toes, I brushed my lips against his.

The tiny peck I had planned to give Shaw quickly turned into more as he took control of the kiss. He took full advantage of my lips parting on a gasp, his tongue sliding between them to explore the depths of my mouth as it tangled with mine. One of his hands slid up my back to tangle in my hair while the other lifted so he could cup my cheek. Tilting my head back, he deepened the kiss, only pulling away when someone rapped their knuckles against the door and called, "Is it safe to come in?"

"Fucking hell," Shaw groaned. "You're dangerous to my self-control, baby."

I fanned myself with my hand as he strode across the room to open the door. The heat in my cheeks was from a mixture of the first passion I'd ever experienced and being embarrassed to have basically been caught making out.

Molly grinned at him, wagging her brows when she bumped him out of the way to walk over to me. I had met the VP's wife the last time I was at the Iron Rogues clubhouse, but we hadn't interacted much back then. So I was surprised when she gave me a hug and murmured, "Welcome back. I know the circumstances aren't ideal, but it's so good to see you again, Britta."

I flashed her a weak smile. "You, too."

Molly turned toward Shaw. "Mav wanted me to tell you to get your ass moving since the meeting is going to be in your office. Don't worry about Britta. Since she mostly hung out with her mom who was stuck in bed recuperating the last time she was here, she didn't get to see much, so I'll show her around."

He heaved a deep sigh and crossed the room

again, shrugging his leather vest off his broad shoulders. "Wear this when you're not in my room."

There was a mischievous glint in Molly's eyes as she said, "Your cut is going to hang down to her knees, Stone."

"Don't have a problem with that," he grunted, quirking a brow at her.

"Even though she's perfectly safe at the clubhouse?" she prodded with a laugh.

He tugged my arms into the holes of the vest and settled it into place on my back before staring into my eyes and murmuring, "I'm gonna make it so you're safe wherever you are. Nobody will ever mess with you again, baby."

"Okay," I breathed, believing every word of his vow.

He gave me another quick kiss before turning to Molly. "Take care of my girl."

"Will do," she promised.

We watched him stalk out of the room, and then Molly slapped my shoulder. "Hot damn! I was starting to think we'd be stuck with asshole Stone forever, but then you got here, and I'm already seeing glimpses of the guy who used to smile and joke around all the time. Although I doubt he'll ever be totally laid back again now that he's turning into an overprotective Neanderthal like my old man and the other brothers who've found their old ladies."

It was hard to believe that being away from me had that kind of an impact on Shaw. But maybe he really had missed me as much as I had him. "You got all of that from him wanting me to wear his cut?"

"I've been around to get a front-row seat to what happens when these guys fall hard." Looping her elbow with mine, she guided me out of Shaw's room, pausing to make sure the door locked behind us. "So you can trust that I know what I'm talking about when I say that he's gonna have you practically surrounded by bubble wrap until this mess with your mom is cleared up. And he won't be much better once that's all sorted."

I got similar comments from the other women as Molly showed me around the clubhouse. Not much had changed in the two years since I had been here, except for the number of women and children who were part of the club.

Smiling at the newest addition, I asked, "So you just recently got married to Viper?"

"Yup," she confirmed with a smile, resting her hand over her still-flat belly. "And he knocked me up already."

"Of course he did." Alice, Deviant's wife, was

sitting close enough to her on the couch that she was able to bump shoulders. "It's an Iron Rogue tradition, after all."

Looking at her slightly rounded belly, I laughed. "One that's safe to assume your husband took very seriously."

She pointed at her belly. "Yeah, and he does nothing by half measures, which is probably how I ended up with twins. And why he bragged about it as soon as we got the news."

"Wow, congratulations!" I tilted my glass of cranberry juice toward her with a grin.

"Thanks." She took a sip of her drink and muttered, "It would have been nice to be able to toast my own wedding with champagne, but at least Grady more than made up for it later that night."

The other women sent her knowing looks, but I ducked my head, my cheeks burning. This was all so new to me. I'd never really had girl talk like this before since Izzy had been a virgin who'd never been on a date either when I last talked to her. And I had just had my first kiss only an hour ago.

"Sorry, Britta," Alice apologized. "You'd think as one of the newer old ladies, I would remember what it's like when you're first getting to know each other while falling for your man."

I tucked a lock of my hair behind my ear, my cheeks filling with heat at being the center of attention. "Oh, um...I really like Shaw, but we...um... barely know each other. So I'm not sure—"

Molly interrupted me to say, "You might not be sure what's happening between the two of you yet. But I am. You're sitting there wearing Stone's cut and using his first name. That's all the proof I need to tell you to get ready to be claimed by your very own Iron Rogue."

5

STONE

To my frustration, the meeting wasn't going to be a short one. It was necessary, but that didn't stop me from being irritated and grouchy.

We'd been vague about our assumptions in front of Britta. However, when Fox arrived in my office, I didn't hesitate to verbalize it. "We have a fucking leak."

He nodded and walked over to sit on the edge of my desk. "Don't know how else someone would discover their location. Deviant and I buried that shit deep."

"I know." I tried to keep the resentment out of my tone, but I was still salty over his refusal to share the information with me.

Fox narrowed his eyes in warning, so I backed off

before I ended up with his gun pointed at me. Then Maverick and several of my brothers walked in, halting our conversation anyway.

"Gotta be a motherfucking rat," Maverick snarled.

"What did King have to say?" Whiskey asked as he took a position against the wall to the right of the door.

"Pissed as fuck," Fox replied. "Had to be one of his guys because I kept the Iron Rogues far away from anything involving B and Marylin."

"Britta," I grated out, gritting my teeth.

Fox raised an eyebrow in question.

"Her name is Britta. Nobody but me calls her anything else."

Fox pressed his lips together as if holding back a smile, and I narrowed my eyes. He cleared his throat and continued, "I kept them far away from *Britta* and her mother. King trusts his patches like I do you, so we're confident it's a prospect. Just need to find a way to smoke him out."

"Francesco's plant should be able to help with that," I told them. "Probably easiest if we get them on a conference call rather than speculating what they can or might do. Get us all on the same page right away."

Fox gave me a chin lift, indicating I should go forward with that plan.

Both men happened to be available, so we hashed things out for the next few hours. Without knowing much right then, we couldn't do a whole lot until Francesco's inside man or King's investigation yielded some information.

I was fucking exhausted when I trudged down the hallway to my room. But I also felt lighter than I had in years. Britta was finally with me, in my arms and in my bed, and I was never letting her go.

The room was mostly dark when I entered, but I could see just enough from the partially closed door to the bathroom since Britta had left the light on in there. It probably made me a fucking pussy, but the fact that she'd been so considerate had warmth blooming in my chest.

She slept curled up in the center of the bed, her cheek resting on one pillow, with her gorgeous blond hair spread out behind her. Her curvy body was wrapped around my other pillow, and I smiled, thinking that she was using it as a substitute for me. Especially when she hugged it tighter and inhaled deeply before settling back down.

Damn, she was cute. And so fucking sexy that I'd

been rock hard since the minute I saw her earlier in the day.

Before I met Britta, it had been years since I'd felt even a passing interest in a woman. But she brought out a side of me that I hadn't even known was there.

After the incident during my first year out of law school, I'd built a wall around myself. It had been the only way to keep all the anguish and rage contained inside me. Since then, only my brothers have been able to penetrate it, but they couldn't even break the shell completely.

I knew Britta would smash it to pieces. Maybe that should've scared the shit out of me, but it didn't. The fear that I might let her down was still there, and it would probably drive her batshit crazy that I was so overprotective, but as long as she knew I loved her without limits, I had no doubt she'd put up with my caveman attitude.

She'd have to get used to it because there was nothing that I wouldn't do to keep her.

I'd never felt such an overwhelming need—to fuck her, to keep her safe. Hell, just to fucking be around her.

I couldn't take my eyes off her while I stripped out of my clothes. As much as I wanted to wake

Britta with my hands and mouth all over her, I could see the darkness under her eyes, and her expression was pained.

I left the bathroom light on so I could stare at my beautiful girl. Pulling back the covers, I couldn't help smiling when I noticed she was wearing one of my shirts. I slipped in behind her and wrapped her up in my arms and legs. She immediately released the pillow and turned over to curl against my chest with a cute little sigh.

She was going to fucking kill me with sounds like that. I sighed and told my dick to stand down so I could try to get a little rest.

"Shaw?" she whispered sleepily.

"Go back to sleep, baby. You need your rest."

"Did you figure out who the mole is?"

"What?" I asked, surprised at her question. How had she known?

"You guys are adorable trying to protect me from being scared, so I let you. But it was pretty obvious that the only way they could have found us was if there was a leak in the organization."

"Damn, I obviously underestimated you, baby," I said with a grin. Then I grimaced. "But I don't think anyone would describe us as adorable."

Britta giggled. "Cute, then?"

"Fucking hell, baby. You're making a bunch of badass bikers sound like teddy bears."

"Maybe I was only referring to you," she replied softly. "I probably should have said hot or sexy as sin or something like that, but...um..."

"Yeah?" I encouraged her when it sounded as though she might not continue.

"Well, you...um...have a cute butt."

I couldn't help it. I tossed my head back and laughed, but I tried to squelch it quickly when she buried her face in my chest. I didn't want to make her feel any more embarrassed because I loved her honesty.

"Hey," I said softly, tugging on a few strands of her hair to bring her head back so I could see her face. "You don't ever have to feel embarrassed about anything that happens between us." I grinned again and winked at her as my hand traveled down to skip under her shirt and palm her ass. "You are cute as hell, baby. But you're also fucking gorgeous and so sexy all I can think about is finally being inside you."

Britta sucked in a quick breath, and her hands splayed on my chest, the heat from her palms practically searing my flesh. "Me too," she whispered so quietly I almost didn't hear her.

My hand clenched her ass cheek, and my hips

involuntarily bucked into her. "Don't say shit like that to me right now, Britta," I growled. "I'm barely hanging on as it is."

"Why?"

I exhaled roughly. "Because you're tired. It's been a long, terrifying day. And because I should take you on at least one fucking date before I pop your cherry."

Britta gasped. "How did you...?"

"You radiate innocence," I muttered as I dropped my head into the crook of her neck and shoulder. After taking a deep inhale, I sighed. "And I can practically smell your sweet little cherry, baby." It was probably just my imagination, but it seemed like I could also smell her ripe, unprotected womb. Just waiting for me to stuff it full of my seed and put my baby inside her.

"Oh," she squeaked as a shiver wracked her body.

"Now go to sleep," I grunted, barely hanging on to my sanity.

Britta wiggled closer, and I growled in warning. Then she rubbed her nose against my chest and sighed. "You make me feel so safe. But I'm still scared. Do you think you could distract me?"

"You're playing with fire, baby," I rasped.

She traced my tattoos for a minute, then kissed my chest, before making me almost come up off the bed when she licked the barbell in my left nipple. "I want to burn," she breathed.

"Fuck," I grunted as every rational thought in my head was replaced by desire. The need to be inside her, to claim her, to own her. I was desperate to hear her scream my name while I exploded inside her.

My lips crashed down onto hers, and I rolled her onto her back before settling myself on top of her. Her generous tits pillowed against my chest, and her hard little nipples poked through her shirt.

At first, I held her head so it was at just the right angle for me to deepen the kiss and plunder her mouth. But soon, my hands itched to caress her curves, and I slowly glided them down to the bottom of the shirt, which had risen to her waist.

I tore my mouth from hers just long enough to whip the T-shirt over her head and toss it away. Then I kissed her again and filled my hands with her tits while rocking my hard-on into the apex of her thighs.

She moaned, and her legs curled around my calves.

"You want me inside you, Britta?"

She nodded.

"Want me to fill you with my big, fat cock and make you come until you're screaming with ecstasy?"

She nodded again, so I pinched her nipples hard, making her gasp.

"Tell me, baby. Tell me you want me to fuck you and take that cherry you've been saving for me."

"Yes, Shaw," she moaned.

"Yes, what?" I ground my pelvis into hers and teased her tight peaks with my fingers.

"I want you. Please, Shaw, take me."

"Who do you belong to, Britta?"

"You," she breathed.

"Damn straight."

I slid a hand down her stomach until I reached the silky fabric of her panties. With one yank, I ripped them away and raised them to my nose, inhaling deeply. "Fuck, you smell delicious." My mouth watered, and I groaned, "Need a taste. Want you on my tongue when I pop your cherry."

Slowly, I trailed my tongue down her body as I moved to lay between her legs. I pushed them wide open and wedged my shoulders into her thighs.

My hands slid beneath her ass, and I raised her pelvis to my mouth. "Smells even better with my face in your pussy." She was bare, and it was sexy as fuck, especially since it didn't hide how wet she was.

Her arousal glistened on her puffy petals, and my tongue darted out to lick up a few drops. The flavor exploded on my taste buds, and I groaned.

I dragged my tongue up Britta's center, and she cried out, her legs tightening against my shoulders.

Burying my face in her pussy, I alternated between licking and fucking her with my tongue, staying away from her clit. Her hips undulated, begging for more every time I backed off.

Her hands tunneled into my hair, and she whimpered in desperate need. I stared up at her as I devoured her and saw the lost expression on her face. "Shaw, please," she begged. "I need..."

She shook her head and clenched her fingers, tugging so hard it was painful, but it only fueled the burn.

It was clear that she didn't have any idea what she was reaching for. The fact that I was about to give her first orgasm made me want to beat against my chest and shout that this woman was mine in every way.

I was going to be her first everything...and her last.

When Britta was nearly out of her mind with need, I finally concentrated my efforts on her sensitive little bud.

"Shaw!" she gasped before she screamed in bliss.

To my shock, she gushed into my mouth, and I drank down every delicious drop. Fuck, my woman was incredibly passionate. And yeah, I was damn smug that she responded to me with such intensity.

"What? I..."

Her expression was horrified, and I gave her a crooked smile. "You are sexy as fuck, baby. And so damn passionate, you squirted. I'm already addicted to the taste."

"That's, um, normal?"

I shook my head. "Not every woman can do it. Even the ones who can have to be with the right man."

Britta's lips tipped up. "Feeling pretty proud about that?"

"Fuck yes," I agreed before going back to eating her pussy.

When she was close, I inserted a finger in her channel. Her muscles spasmed around it, and I grunted, "Damn, baby, you're so tight." I was a big man, and that included the rock-hard monster aching to be inside her. If I didn't want to hurt Britta any more than necessary, I needed her to be soft and stretched.

After pushing her into another hard climax, I

was able to fit three fingers. But I wasn't going to last any longer. I was already making a mess of the sheets with the come leaking from my dick.

Keeping our bodies pressed together, I glided up until we were face-to-face, and my hips settled snugly between her legs, my cock pulsing between the lips of her pussy.

Britta's hands came to rest on my biceps, and she shuddered when I took her mouth in a deep, wet kiss. I curled my hands under her thighs and lifted them, setting her feet on the mattress with her knees bent. The position opened her even wider, and the angle made it easy for me to push the tip of my cock inside her.

Fucking hell. She was like a fucking furnace, and her inner walls squeezed me so hard I nearly came right then.

I sucked in a breath and fought for control. "No going back now, baby," I murmured when I pulled back from her lips. "You're mine."

My hips surged forward, breaking through her barrier and filling her from root to tip. "Fuck!" I shouted at the same time that she cried out. It took every bit of my strength, but I kept still while she adjusted to me.

I kissed away the tears dripping from her pain-filled eyes. "Relax, baby. It will pass, I promise."

Britta took a deep breath, and the movement caused her body to rock against mine. Her eyes widened, and she gasped, "Oh!"

I smirked. "Feeling better?"

She nodded, and then her cheeks turned crimson. "Can you...um...move?"

"Like this?" I asked as I pulled back just an inch before seating myself fully once more.

"Yesss," she moaned, her eyes closing and her fingers digging into my flesh.

"Eyes open, baby," I demanded. "Want you to watch me make you come. Know who owns this sexy little body."

This time, I retreated until only the tip remained inside her before thrusting deep. I groaned at the streaks of pleasure that shot through my body. Britta buried her face in my neck, muffling her cry of pleasure.

"Don't," I rasped.

"Huh?" Her eyes were glazed with lust as she stared up at me in confusion.

"Don't hide from me. Or keep me from hearing what I do to you." I grunted as I pulled out and drove back in. "Want to hear every moan, every sigh. Want to hear you screaming my name."

"Shaw," she breathed when I filled her once more.

Her fevered expression and raspy tone sent me over the edge. Grasping the sheets on both sides of her, I dug my knees into the mattress for leverage and slammed inside her so deep my cock bumped her cervix.

An image of Britta's naked body round and swollen with my baby flashed in my mind. Then nothing remained except the determination to make her come so hard her womb took in everything I gave it.

I pounded in and out of her over and over, making the springs on the bed squeak and the headboard slam into the wall.

"Fuck! That's it, baby! Take it. Oh fuck, yeah! Fuck!"

Britta's tits bounced with every thrust, and I bent my head to suck on a stiff peak. I used the fingers of one hand to twist and pluck the other before switching.

"Shaw," Britta moaned. "Oh, yes. Yes!"

Her eyes began to close but flew open when I snarled, "Eyes!"

My gaze drifted down to watch my giant dick disappear into her tight pussy, coming out shiny with her juices. "You have no idea how fucking sexy it is to watch you take my cock like such a good girl."

I locked eyes with her again and fucked her even faster and deeper as one of my hands journeyed down her slick skin to her pussy.

"Gonna squirt for me again," I commanded. I kissed her, pouring all of my need into it. Then I muttered, "Wanna hear you scream my name, baby."

"Yesss," she whimpered.

After a few more thrusts, I pressed my thumb on her pleasure button, rubbing it hard. A second later, her back bowed, and she screamed my name as she flew into a mind-blowing orgasm.

"Oh fuck, baby! Squeeze that pussy! Fuck, yes! Fuck!" I roared as my climax crashed over me, and come erupted from my dick.

I continued to plunge in and out, prolonging her pleasure with my still rock-hard cock. "One more time," I growled.

When she detonated a second time, I felt the gush of her arousal soaking my dick and sending me spiraling into another climax.

"Holy shit," I panted when the ability to speak returned.

"Yeah," Britta mumbled through choppy breathing.

I grinned and buried my face in her neck, putting a soft kiss on her damp skin. "You're amazing."

Raising my head, I winked at her when I saw her flushed cheeks.

I gave her a hard kiss, then slowly withdrew. "Stay here, baby."

"Mm-hmm." She closed her eyes and sighed as her limbs fell like a limp noodle.

Chuckling, I climbed out of bed and ducked into the bathroom to clean up and grab a warm, wet cloth. Then I returned and gently wiped away the remnants of our pleasure and her virginity.

I tried not to gloat at the pink stain on the washcloth but obviously failed.

"Molly was right," Britta sassed. "You guys are Neanderthals."

Unrepentant, I shrugged and tossed the cloth into the hamper before crawling back into bed and pulling her into my arms. "Sleep, baby."

6

BRITTA

Waking up in Shaw's bed with my cheek resting on one of his biceps and his muscular thigh wedged between my legs was an amazing way to start the morning. Although, judging by the pink tone of the sunlight peeking through the blinds covering the window, it was still super early.

The only thing better than being wrapped up in my sexy biker like this would've been if my mom was safe.

I knew she would be thrilled I was with Shaw since she knew how much I had thought about him over the past two years. But that didn't stop me from struggling a little with being so happy when she was out there somewhere, possibly fighting for her life.

I was pulled out of my thoughts when Shaw

mumbled something under his breath, his hold on me tightening. Twisting my neck to look up at him, I found his eyes screwed shut, his brow wrinkled, and his lips pressed into a flat line. I reached up to smooth his forehead, gently swiping my fingertip across the line that had popped up in the middle.

"No," he shouted, wrapping his fingers around my wrist to stop me.

Before he could tighten his grip, I said, "It's me, Britta."

At the sound of my voice, his eyes popped open. He had been deep asleep only a second before, but there was no haziness in his blue orbs when he looked at our hands, his hold gentling. "Fuck, baby. I didn't hurt you, did I?"

"No," I rushed to assure him as he turned my wrist from side to side, checking for any sign that he had held me too hard. When he saw for himself that there weren't any marks on my skin, I added, "You seemed like you were having a bad dream, so I went to smooth your brow, but it didn't help. My touch startled you instead."

"It wasn't anything you did," he reassured me, shifting our positions so we rested on our sides facing each other. Then he lifted my hand and pressed a kiss against the inside of my wrist. "I've been battling with nightmares for a damn long time, and the feel of your fingers against my skin pulled me out a fuck of a lot faster than anything else has ever done."

I loved that I was able to help him, even if only a little bit. But that didn't make me feel much better. "I hate that you've struggled like that. What are your nightmares about?"

"I saw some shit overseas that I can't seem to get outta my head." He heaved a deep sigh, settling his hand on my hip. "And there was a situation that went sideways." He looked reluctant to talk about it, and I wondered what it would take to get him to open up to me. "Anyway, I tend to bottle this shit up, hiding behind smiles and jokes, but I can't do that when I'm asleep. That's when it all bubbles up."

I cupped his cheek with my palm, the bristle of his scruff scraping against my skin. "You know that you can tell me anything, right? I don't want you to feel like you have to keep stuff from me when you're struggling. I get that you can't share some things because of club business, but I don't want there to be other secrets between us. I'll understand if you aren't ready yet, though. If you want to wait until we know each other better..."

"I think we've waited more than long enough already, don't you?" He stroked his thumb against my waist, and even with the sheet between us, his touch left goose bumps in its wake. "The past two years were torture, not being able to see you were safe with my own eyes."

Butterflies swirled in my belly at his words. "You thought about me too?"

"All the damn time, baby." He fisted the sheet in his hand. "Can't tell you how many times I almost went up against my prez for keeping your location a secret. Drove me up the fucking wall when you turned eighteen, and I couldn't come to you."

My lips curved into a satisfied smile. "Good."

"Now, who's smug?" he teased.

"Maybe a little." I lifted my hand to squeeze my thumb and forefinger until they were less than an inch from each other. "I would be even more so if you wanted to share with me what's torturing you so much that you have nightmares so many years after you left the military."

He raked his fingers through his hair with a deep sigh. "Do me a favor and don't ever use those pretty green eyes of yours for evil. It's damn hard to tell you no when you look at me like that."

I blinked at him, pasting an innocent expression on my face. "I promise to only use my puppy dog eyes for good...except for when you want me to be bad."

"Quit being so damn perfect so I can get this out, and then we can move on to much better things to talk about," he grumbled, a serious gleam entering his eyes.

"I don't think the average person realizes that military lawyers still get sent overseas to serve. We don't just spend our days behind the safety of a desk," he explained. "And no matter how much training I got at Judge Advocate General school, nothing truly prepares you to translate book knowledge to what I encountered over there."

I stroked my hand down his chest, then traced my finger over the dragon tattoo on his right pec. "I can't even imagine."

"I don't want you to," he growled, dipping his head to brush his lips over mine. "You're the light after all the darkness even though I don't deserve you."

"I love that you think of me that way, but I disagree. I think you deserve me very much."

His lips curved up slightly, the strain in his expression easing a little. "Which is damn lucky for me since your opinion is the only one that matters."

I winked at him. "And don't you forget it."

"Hopefully having your light shine on me will help me forget the life that was lost because of me." I kept stroking his chest, hoping to offer him some comfort while he struggled with getting his story out. "There was a group of hostages who had been taken. I can't tell you where or when because that would be crossing a line. But I can say that my commanding officer needed to buy some time for the covert team to get in place to infiltrate so they could safely extract everyone. A negotiator wasn't available, and they couldn't get one there fast enough. The timeline was so fucking tight because a couple of the hostages were in bad shape. It was a situation where minutes counted, so he asked me to give it a try since I was their best bet at keeping the bad guys distracted long enough to get the job done."

"I can understand why he chose you with how good you are with words," I murmured.

"Yeah, well that didn't do me much good because they brought one of the hostages with them." A muscle jumped in his jaw. "We weren't expecting it, and things went even more to shit from there. I tried to get him out myself in the chaos, but I was outnumbered. We both got shot, and I thought for sure that was the end for me. But one of the covert guys showed up just in time to save my life. Only mine, though. The hostage was already dead, and we couldn't even take his body with us. Leaving him behind is what truly haunts me. He had a family in the States who never got to bury him."

I pressed a kiss against the bullet scar on his shoulder, grateful he had made it out alive. "I'm so sorry."

"Me too." His smile held no humor, only regret. "Not that it does much good for his wife or daughter."

"You're not responsible for the hostage's death." I twined my arms around his neck. "You tried your best to help them, but sometimes the odds are stacked against you. Just like I've felt like they've been for me my entire life until I met you."

"I have a fuck of a lot of regrets, but I am so damn grateful that the shit I went through finally led me here. To you."

I drifted my hand lower to tug on the barbell piercing in his nipple. Shaw was the best distraction for my worry about my mom. Maybe I could be the same for him and get rid of his nightmares.

7

STONE

It was two days before anyone found something for us to put our plans in motion. One thing we discovered was that Tommaso had been charged with murder and was currently in jail without parole. When it came to Marylin, that news could be bad or worse.

They might have snatched Britta's mom and were holding her until Tommaso was released. Deviant said this would happen soon because the evidence against Tommaso was circumstantial and the key witness had just disappeared. Or they'd taken Marilyn simply to get rid of her, and she was already dead.

As much as I hated to keep shit from my woman, I didn't think sharing that information would do any good. It was all speculation at this point anyway. So I filed it away as club business in my mind.

Britta had already been plagued with worry and despair, but she'd tried to hide it. I still managed to distract her more often than not. Not just with sex—although we fucked like bunnies—but by showing her around town, telling her more about club life, and getting to know each other better.

Britta had quickly become my emotional safe space. My nightmares hadn't been as intense after that first night, and I had a feeling that with her in my bed, they might go away completely someday.

We were cuddled up in the lounge, talking with a few of my brothers and their old ladies when my phone rang. It was on the end table beside me, so I reached over and picked it up. The number was one that I memorized so that it wasn't written down anywhere or saved in my phone—Francesco's private line.

I flashed the screen at Whiskey, who immediately pulled his phone from the inner pocket of his cut and sent a text.

"Gotta take this, baby," I murmured to Britta before kissing her temple and pushing to my feet.

"Stone," I answered as I walked toward my office.

Neither of us bothered with pleasantries.

"Carlos checked in. Apparently, he managed to get Darius smashed. Carlos didn't want to endanger his cover if the asshole happened to remember their conversation, so he was cagey with his questions. Darius is definitely aware of the situation. He confirmed that they were holding—I won't use his language—someone who'd been hiding from them. Unfortunately, he doesn't know where Miss Hughes is."

"Fuck," I muttered.

So far, Deviant and Grey had both struck out when it came to finding Marylin. They'd followed the trail, but eventually it just ended. As if it'd simply ceased to exist. They were monumentally pissed about it, and both their egos were smarting over it.

"One positive is that by Darius telling Carlos he didn't know where she was being held, he essentially confirmed that she's still alive."

He had a point. We had no idea what condition she was in or what was being done to her, but she was alive.

"However," Francesco continued, "it's looking more like they're holding her for Tommaso."

"So we need to get to her before he's released."

"That would be my assumption as well. Unfortunately, Carlos heard this morning that Tommaso's lawyer managed to get the case transferred to a judge they control. The case goes before him in two days, and if he isn't able to get it thrown out, the judge will most certainly release Tommaso on bail."

"Son of a bitch," I cursed, holding the phone so tight it was just luck that it didn't crack.

My gaze was on the ceiling until I heard people entering my office. Whiskey walked in with Maverick, Deviant, and Hunter right behind him. Fox was home with his wife and sick twins, but the VP would fill him in later.

"Anything new on Portia?"

"No. I—" He stopped speaking for a beat, then went on. "Actually, Carlos did say something about her. It didn't seem significant, so I almost forgot about it. However, maybe I'm overlooking something. It seems Darius is quite bitter over the fact that he hasn't been able to get into Portia's bed. But Carlos got the impression from several people that her bedroom has a revolving door."

"Is Darius an exception, or does she avoid sleeping with the people she works with?"

"I didn't ask. Do you think it's important? If so, I'll get a message to Carlos."

"Could be. Not quite sure how yet. But my instincts are telling me to find out."

"I'll get back to you as soon as I have an answer."

"Thanks."

"Of course. *Ciao.*"

After hanging up, I filled my brothers in on what I'd learned from Francesco. While they discussed what I'd told them, my eyes drifted around my office. It was almost as big as the prez's and VP's because nearly three-quarters of the walls were taken up by bookshelves.

The books were all meticulously arranged in the order that made it easier for me to find what I needed. Because the majority of them were law books.

You're a fucking lawyer, dipshit.

"Deviant," I called, interrupting the conversation. "Get me all the files involved in Tommaso's case."

He raised his brow but nodded. "Sure."

I was already out of my chair and scanning a particular set of books as I gave orders. "The rest of you touch base with King. Give him what we know to see if it helps with his angle."

"Think there's a legal solution to keep Tommaso in jail?" Hunter guessed.

"Possibly. But it's a long shot," I admitted as I grabbed several large volumes and dropped them onto my desk.

"Text you when I send the files," Deviant told me before exiting the office.

The others turned to follow him, but I called out to Maverick, who stopped and pivoted.

"The Chicago chapter have a lawyer?" I asked.

He thought for a minute, scratching the side of his jaw. "Not a patch. But I think one of the officers has a sister with a law degree."

"Have her get in touch with me. Even if I figure something out, I might not be able to handle it from here. But I'm not leaving Britta unless we're ready to bring Tommaso and the boss to The Room."

"Done." He jerked his chin up and down once, then left.

I could do a few things before I got the information from Deviant, but I decided to go find my girl.

Less than an hour later, Britta and I were in the kitchen rustling up some dinner when my phone chirped with a text from Deviant.

DEVIANT

Sent the files.

ME

Thanks

DEVIANT

It's a lot to sort through, but I figured it couldn't hurt to get the files for the dirty judge too.

ME

Good thinking.

Damn, that was going to be a fuck ton of information to go through. There was no way I could do it on my own.

"What do you want to drink?" Britta inquired, drawing me out of my thoughts.

"I'll get the drinks, baby. Go sit and relax."

Britta sighed, but the corners of her mouth lifted slightly. "Telling me to relax doesn't make me actually relax, you know."

I grabbed a beer and a sparkling water from the fridge before answering her as I walked to the table. "Yeah, but it's my job to take care of you, so I'll keep trying."

"I'd rather have something to do," she muttered. "I love spending time with you, but I'm going a little stir-crazy. Especially when there's nothing I can do to help my mom."

An idea began to form, but before I could put much thought into it, my phone rang. It was Francesco again.

"I'm sorry, baby," I apologized with a grimace. "I need to take this in my office."

"Okay," she said sweetly, without a trace of anything except understanding in her voice.

"You're fucking perfect, baby," I told her before heading toward the kitchen door.

"You can prove it to me later," she called out, making me chuckle and get hard at the same time.

"Give me a second. I'm almost to my office." Once I was inside, with the door firmly closed, I sat in my desk chair and put the phone to my ear again. "That was fast."

"Carlos was in a situation that made it possible for him to answer right away," Francesco explained. "From what he's seen, Portia only spends significant amounts of time in bed with people who are above her—*perdono*, no pun intended. But from gossip—which means the accuracy is questionable, but I still thought we should take it into account—she generally uses her body to get information or other things that she wants. It has me wondering..."

He trailed off, and I picked up his line of thought. "If she found out where Britta and Marylin were by fucking the right people?"

"Yes, but I can't find the connection."

"I'll put Deviant and Grey on it, and in the

meantime, I'm gonna talk to King and see if it strikes a chord with him."

We ended the call, and I mused over what I'd learned for a few minutes, then called Deviant and Gray to fill them in. I decided to put off my conversation with King until tomorrow and get back to Britta.

"Everything okay?" she asked, trying not to look anxious.

The idea that had occurred to me earlier had been percolating, and I'd decided it was a good solution. Even though it would require telling Britta some shit I'd hoped to shield her from.

"Actually, we got some new information today." Britta's face brightened, and I hated that I was going to chase that hopeful expression away. I stood and moved to her chair, lifted her into my arms, then sat and settled her on my lap.

"I wanted to spare you the details until I had something concrete to tell you," I admitted reluctantly. "But the truth is, I could use your help. It would give you something to do, and you'd be helping us to find your mom and get these assholes taken care of once and for all."

Britta sat up and stared at me eagerly. "Seriously? I can help?"

I shared almost everything we knew, without

divulging things that needed to remain club business. To my surprise, she wasn't the least bit angry with me for withholding.

"I get it," she sighed. "I want to help, but it was better for my nerves when I wasn't sure that they were planning to kill my mom."

"At least we know she's still alive, baby," I reminded her gently.

She looked at her lap and nodded. Then she met my eyes, and my heart squeezed painfully at the fear and anguish in her green pools. "You know he's going to beat her to death if he gets the chance, right?"

"I won't let it come to that," I promised her. I was gonna make sure Tommaso had the same fate he was planning for Marylin. Except I knew how to draw it out, to make it as painful as possible. Before I let him die, he'd wish that he'd never touched a woman in anger.

"Let's go to bed, and I'll explain how you can help."

I told her about all the files that needed to be combed through and why. She might not have any training in law, but with some guidance, I knew she was smart enough to spot what I was looking for.

When we'd shed our clothes and got into bed, she kissed me softly and whispered, "Thank you."

Before I could respond, she kissed me again, but this time it was full of passion. Then she straddled me and rode my cock like a wild woman until she was gushing on my dick, soaking it so I slid in and out with ease. After giving her two screaming orgasms, I finally let go and filled her to the brim with my come.

She collapsed on top of me and was asleep seconds later. So fucking adorable.

I maneuvered us so that we were both on our sides. Then I pulled her against me and wrapped my body around hers.

The nightmares didn't wake me that night. But her sexy little ass wiggling against my cock did. Groaning, I lifted her leg and draped it over mine, opening her up so I could slide into her tight pussy. She moaned and pressed her ass back against me every time my hips bucked, driving me deeper inside her. I palmed her big, sexy tits, squeezing them and playing with her diamond hard nipples.

It wasn't long before we both reached completion, shouting in ecstasy as we dove off the cliff together.

I fell back asleep still buried inside her.

8

BRITTA

Being able to lend Shaw a hand meant the world to me, especially since it meant that I was doing something to help my mom. Even if it was just sorting through a ridiculous number of documents, hoping to find some clue to help the Iron Rogues find her. We'd been at it for hours this morning, but no luck yet.

On the plus side, though, watching Shaw work made me wish that I had the chance to see him in action in court someday. I shivered a little, thinking about how sexy he would be.

"What was that for?" he asked, proving that he was too observant for me to get away with much of anything.

"Just picturing what you'd look like in a courtroom, dressed in a three-piece suit while you dazzled a jury with your brilliance." I wagged my brows. "There ought to be a law against you being so hot."

"You think I'm hot, huh?" he drawled, setting down the stack of papers he'd been reading through.

"Obviously," I drawled. "The hottest."

He stood and prowled toward me. "It's good you think so since you're not gonna get another, less hot guy now that you're mine."

It really turned me on when he got all growly and possessive. Pressing my thighs to better ease the ache in my core, I let out a surprised yelp when he scooped me out of my chair. Wrapping my legs around his waist, I held on while he walked us over to the door. I thought he was planning to carry me to his room, but he locked it, then pressed my back against the hard surface instead.

As I gripped his shoulders, he fused our lips together in a deep kiss, our tongues tangling. The muscles in his arms bulged as he lifted me higher and I tilted my head so he could take it even deeper. Just like the other times we'd kissed, it wasn't long before things got heated.

I hadn't brought a lot of clothes with me, and I hadn't done laundry yet, so Shaw had given me one of his shirts to wear. I wished that I hadn't bothered to put on my jeans as well, except he'd made it very clear that I shouldn't ever walk around half dressed near anyone but him. But if I were just in his shirt and a pair of panties, it would've given him easier access when he slid his hand between us.

"You wet for me, baby?" he rasped, trailing kisses down my jawline.

"Uh-huh," I breathed, wiggling my hips to shift back a little so he could undo the snap on my jeans.

When he got the zipper down, he tried to slide his hand inside, but our positions didn't give him enough room. Frustrated, he growled, "Gotta get you naked."

I unwound my legs from his waist, and he set me on my feet. Then he made quick work of stripping my jeans down my legs and taking my panties with them. Once that was done, he reached under my shirt—which was huge on me—to undo my bra to get access to my tits.

"Gonna make you come on my tongue," he muttered, picking me up again and placing hot, open-mouthed kisses down the column of my neck.

"Yes, please," I hissed, more than ready to have his mouth on me again even though that was how I'd woken up this morning.

Lifting me again, he backed me against the door

and slid one of his hands beneath my shirt. Since it was so big, there was more than enough room for him to get his head under it too, licking one of my nipples before sucking it into his mouth. It felt as though each tug of his lips sent a direct line of fire to my core.

I cried out and pushed my chest closer as he switched sides, nibbling and sucking on my other nipple before moving down my torso. "Need your pussy."

That was all the warning he gave me before he slid his palms along my outer thighs, all the way to my knees. Taking the hint to unwrap my legs from his waist, I held his neck while he draped them over his bulging biceps. Then he used the wall as leverage to push me high enough that he could get my legs over his shoulders.

My new position was precarious, but I trusted Shaw completely. And my faith in him paid off as he licked my pussy from bottom to top. "Keep a hold on me while I eat your sweet pussy until you can't take it anymore. Then I'm gonna sink my cock balls deep until we're coming together."

He followed through with his promise, devouring me until my thighs shook, and I was screaming his name. "Shaw! Yes, oh yes!"

My orgasm ripped through my body, and if he hadn't been holding me up so securely, I would've fallen to the floor in a heap of satisfaction. Instead, I just pressed my head back against the wall while my body shook with tremors. My fingers dug into his scalp as he ate me through my orgasm. Then he unwound his arms and gripped my butt, sliding me down until I was lined up with his dick.

"Reach down and free my cock, baby," he commanded, his voice thick with need.

I slid my arm between us, flicking the snap of his jeans open and dragging the zipper down. He'd gone commando, so I was able to wrap my hand around his shaft and tug it out.

"Such a good girl."

His praise sent a delicious shiver down my spine. "Now what?"

"Let go, baby. I've got it from here."

He proved how true those words were when he lined his dick up with my core and plunged inside with one forceful thrust of his hips. He'd taken me more times than I could count in the days that I'd been here, but it was still a tight fit. My inner walls clamped around his thick invasion, and I felt the slight burn of his shaft stretching me.

"Always so fucking tight. You need a second?" he

asked, his fingers digging into my skin as he tightened his hold while he stilled.

I wiggled my hips as much as I could, my body going liquid when I realized the pinch of pain had already passed. "Nuh-uh, I need you to follow up on your promise to make us both come—together."

Gently lifting me higher, he slid out. Then he plunged back in on a hard stroke, and a low moan escaped my lips. "That's it, baby. Let me hear what I do to you. My office is soundproofed for security reasons, so nobody is gonna hear you."

"I'm already so close again," I gasped.

"Gimme a second one, Britta," he gritted out, circling his hips to hit just the right spot deep inside me. "We can come together on your third."

"Yes, oh yessss," I cried as another wave of pleasure crested over me.

Now that I had come again, he didn't hold back at all. I was barely able to hold on while he hammered in and out of my tight heat. Over and over again until I felt his dick grow impossibly large. "I'm barely holding on here, baby. You better be close if you want us to go together this time."

"Need just a little more," I panted, doing my best to wiggle my hips in unison with his thrusts. Tightening my legs around his waist, I felt my toes literally curl. Each thrust of his hips sent a shock of pleasure up my spine. "Please."

"Come for me now," he whispered, somehow keeping his hold on me with one hand while he slid the other between us, his thumb circling my clit.

I hung suspended on the edge for a second, and then the combination sent me over. My body clenched around his, milking his release from his dick. I felt the heat of his come jetting into me as he found his own orgasm. When our shudders died down, he slipped out of me and slid my body down until my feet touched the floor.

"Whoa, I had no idea that office sex was so awesome," I mumbled after I caught my breath. "Although maybe it was just because you had me up against the door like that, which I had no idea was even possible."

Bending to grab my panties from the floor, he handed them to me and offered, "Next time, I'll take you on the desk and see if you like it as much."

"I will definitely take you up on that." I crossed the room to grab a tissue and clean up before I shimmied back into my panties and tugged my jeans back on. Then I perched on the edge of his desk. "Pencil it in for our next break."

"Whatever you want, baby," he agreed, shaking his head with a deep laugh.

Being with Shaw, I already had just about everything I ever wanted. The only thing missing was my mom, and I had felt better about her odds now that he had filled me in a little more and given me a way to help.

Over the next several days, Britta and I spent most of our time combing the files that Deviant had acquired.

Then one morning, Britta gasped and called me over to the table where she was working on a laptop. "I think I found something!"

I looked over the notes she'd made and then read the corresponding passages she'd marked.

"Damn, baby," I said as I exhaled. "This might work."

"I even jotted down some law books that I thought might help."

Pulling her into my arms, I murmured, "You're fucking brilliant. Ever think about going to law school?"

Britta giggled, then shrugged. "I don't know. I think having a degree is a good idea, but..." Her face flushed, and she dropped her eyes to my chest.

With one finger under her chin, I lifted her face back up to mine. "But what? After everything I've shared with you and the way you turn into a wild cat when we fuck, you shouldn't be embarrassed to tell me anything."

Britta sighed. "I know, but I can't help it. A lot of women would think I'm crazy. I just...I've always wanted to stay at home with my kids. My mom tried to spend time with me, but she was always working just to make sure we had food on the table."

"Baby, I think that's amazing."

Her beautiful face brightened. "You do?"

"You're going to be an incredible mom."

And soon if I have my way. I'd certainly been working hard at it.

IT TURNED out that Britta had been right. We'd come up with a legal way to tie the judge's hands and refuse bail. Then a not-so-legal way to force him to quit and never practice law again. But I didn't tell Britta that part.

I'd also had the lawyer who helped us in Chicago go to the courthouse and file some papers that wouldn't actually change anything about the case, legally. However, they would throw everyone into a tizzy until they figured that out. And while they did, Tommaso would remain locked up.

It wouldn't delay his release more than a week or two, though.

Carlos kept us updated whenever he had new information, but we were mostly interested whenever he heard or found proof that Marylin was still alive. It looked like our first theory had been correct. They were holding her for Tommaso. If we could only find out where the fuck they'd stashed her.

It was another week before King finally called to tell us he'd finally made progress.

"You're not gonna believe this shit," he growled. "Turns out Portia really did her homework. She had somebody track Britta to Izzy. After they realized her dad was an Iron Rogue, they researched the MC. This was right about the time that they noticed that the number of people within their organization disappearing or being killed had been increasing.

"The prez and VP of an MC aren't a secret, but she left a trail of empty beds in order to find out more. But she had to know that you would never lead anyone to Britta and Marylin."

"Then how the fuck did she get their location?" I snarled.

"I hate to say it, man, but the fact that you all marry your old ladies gave her a leg up. It looks like she found Fox's and Maverick's old ladies are the only ones in the head chapter that have strong ties to another MC."

Frustrated, I ran a hand through my hair. "Shit."

Molly and Dahlia were Mac's daughters, the president of the Silver Saints MC. And they were our connection to the Hounds of Hellfire.

"The Silver Saints are as loyal as they come and as tight-lipped about their organization as we are.

"Not to mention that they have just as ruthless of a reputation. No way did she get to one of them."

"No. But she rolled in the sheets with the president of the Devil's Jesters."

"Son of a bitch!"

The Silver Saints had gone head-to-head with the other MC. The Devil's Jesters were mean bastards who treated their women like garbage and were into all kinds of dirty shit.

"That's how she knew to dig into the pasts of the

old ladies. Any connections she found were explored through cash or sex."

Disgusted, I grunted, "I don't even want to know how many dicks she swallowed to get the information."

"Yeah..." I could practically hear him cringing. "Once they looked into Bridget..."

Mac's wife, Bridget, had grown up on the Hounds of Hellfire compound. The former president was her father. King had taken over when the older man retired.

"All this explanation better be leading to the news that you found out who the rat is," I growled. "Otherwise, all you're doing is guaranteeing that I kick your ass the next time I see you."

"Watch it, Jackson," King barked. "Don't threaten me. You come after the president of another club, and Fox will have your ass."

I grunted, unwilling to verbally acknowledge that he was right.

Then he muttered, "And I did find him."

"He better be fucking dead."

"He doesn't know we're onto him yet."

"Why the fuck not?" I bellowed.

"Because we think with the right bread crumbs, he could get Portia to lead us back to the boss."

"You have forty-eight hours to convince me this will work, or I'm comin' down there and putting a bullet between his eyes."

King was quiet for a moment, then spoke in a low tone laced with warning. "I get that she's your woman, Stone, which is why I've put up with your attitude. And why I'm agreeing to your demand. But don't push your fucking luck."

Then he hung up.

I jumped to my feet and ran my hands through my hair before slamming my fists on the desktop.

I was running out of patience and if we didn't figure something out soon, I was gonna lose my shit—which usually ended with someone dead.

Two days later, Britta and I were working in my office when the door slammed open, and Deviant stalked in, holding an open laptop. "I fucking got her," he grunted before spinning around and going right back out.

What the fuck?

Britta jumped to her feet, but I put a hand on her shoulder to keep her from following him. "Sorry, baby. This could involve club business. Promise to fill you in on anything I can after we're done."

She sighed but nodded and slumped back down

into her chair. I gave her a quick, hard kiss, then hurried after Deviant, ending up in Fox's office.

Deviant repeated his statement and set his computer on the prez's desk.

Fox stood and came around to stand by me so we could both see the screen.

"Seven years ago, Portia Lawrence married Gregory Truitt in Las Vegas. A week later, the marriage was annulled. But in that span of time, she created a new identity. P. Truitt. The only reason I finally stumbled across the marriage was because Grey and I have been combing through her life, everywhere she went, what she did while she was there, who she was with. Anything we could find.

"We followed her trail to Gregory Truitt once we realized that she'd had dinner with him multiple times, and they spent the night together. There was nothing else on her credit card, so on a hunch, I pulled his credit card charges. That's when I found that he'd paid for a package at a little white wedding chapel."

"How did you know he married Portia?" I asked. It was the obvious assumption, but I wasn't going after this woman with nothing but Deviant's hunch.

"Grey has another contact in Vegas. They hunted down the marriage certificate. It was only filed in a tiny courthouse that still hasn't digitized their records. The only way to prove to the rest of the world that you got married is to have the original certificate on hand. But if your sole purpose is to create a fake identity, filing the paperwork in a records hall that no one would ever think to check..."

"Unless two geniuses were ripping apart your life," Fox mused.

"Exactly."

"How does this help us find Marylin?" I asked, trying not to sound impatient.

"This identity, P. Truitt. Obviously, it's not the only one out there. But this one"—he pointed at a document on his screen—"has only ever been used once. It's on the rental document for a house on the south side of Chicago."

"How sure are you about all this?" I queried, not sure whether to let myself hope.

"One hundred percent. We saw a man talking to Portia outside her apartment building one day, but we didn't think much about him since we were so intent on following her. I pulled up the feed from the nearest traffic cameras by the house and ran a search for vehicles that matched any others in all the other footage I'd compiled. I got a hit last night."

He clicked a few keys, and a grid of photos

appeared. It was six across and six down, every single one showing the same license plate.

"Apartment building," Deviant said as he pointed at the first picture. "House. Apartment building. The high-rise where Portia works. The house. The apartment building. The house. The high-rise. I'm telling you, that's where they're keeping Marylin."

"Be ready to ride in an hour," Fox grunted, stomping around his desk and picking up his phone.

"Wait," Deviant said, holding up his hand. "That's not all."

"You found Britta's mom," I muttered. "What else is there?"

"Well, unless you were intending for them to go into hiding again, I figured you'd want to know the identity of the boss."

Fox and I gaped at him.

"We'll need King's leak to confirm it, but yeah, I found him, too."

10

STONE

"Well?" I snapped when Deviant didn't immediately give us the name.

"Tommaso Barone."

"What the fuck?" Fox and I exclaimed at the same time.

"But..."

Deviant gestured to the computer screen. "The boss hides in plain sight. It gives him the edge because people will tell him things that they wouldn't tell 'the boss.'"

"That explains why they would be holding Marylin for him," I observed, scrubbing a hand over my face. "I kept wondering why the boss would care enough to keep a hostage until Tommaso was released. Especially when he didn't report directly to the boss."

Deviant nodded, crossing his arms over his chest and leaning his hip on the desk. "It's under his orders, although no one knows that."

"How did you find this out?" Fox asked, his brow furrowed as he took in this shocking news.

"I followed the paperwork trail and noticed Portia's name on most everything, but a few documents had Tommaso's name. At first, I thought it was because Portia was delegating, but then Grey pointed out that during the four months that Tommaso was incarcerated, another name replaced Tommaso's. Elio Barone."

My eyebrows rose. "His son?"

"Yeah. That got me curious about the car from Portia's parking lot. It's registered to Elio."

I rubbed the back of my head and exhaled slowly as I sifted through all the pieces in my head. "I get that Elio is keeping Britta's mom for his dad, but why has he been visiting the house so much?"

Deviant tried to keep his expression neutral, but I caught his slight wince and narrowed my eyes.

"I talked to King this morning. He finally brought the mole in for questioning." Deviant pursed his lips together, then muttered, "Maybe he should tell you the rest."

"You do realize that I'm seconds away from killing, right?" I seethed, my jaw clenched tight.

Deviant pulled his phone from his pocket and hit a button, then put it on speaker.

"King," he answered.

"Tell Fox and Stone what you found out," Deviant demanded.

King sighed. "You left the dirty work for me, didn't you, asshole?"

Deviant snorted. "You're not within shooting distance."

"For fuck's sake!" I shouted. "Somebody tell me what the fuck i going on!"

"We've been interrogating Tom—the prospect who gave up the girls—since last night. He admitted to sleeping with Portia and giving her details that gave away the location of Britta and her mom. He swore that was it and things were over, but he was obviously hiding something. Apparently, she'd ghosted Tom for a week, then suddenly showed and seduced him again."

"They'd found Britta and taken Marylin," Fox pointed out. "What else did she want from him?"

King was silent for a minute then muttered, "Britta."

"What?" I shouted.

Fox shot me a warning look, and I inhaled slowly, attempting to calm down. "Obviously, King kept Britta's whereabouts to himself or someone would have tried to get to her by now."

I clenched my fists and began pacing. "What does this have to do with Tommaso's son?" I asked, remembering their hesitation when they'd talked about him.

"Tom said that Portia repeatedly tried to get him to divulge Britta's location, but eventually, she had to have realized he didn't know. In all her time with Tom, she'd been very careful, but this time, she slipped. He overheard her on the phone later that night. She was pitching a fit about following the person's orders, saying that he was just the boss's son and she didn't answer to him."

"So Deviant is right," Fox surmised. "Tommaso is the one running the organization."

"Yeah," Deviant agreed. "That's what Tom suspected, but he didn't know for sure until the next day when Elio turned up at his apartment. He used his fists to try to convince Tom to tell him what he wanted to know. All the while, Portia complained that his efforts were pointless and that she didn't understand why Tommaso and Elio were so obsessed with these women. Then she accused Elio of wanting to fuck both of them since he'd been visiting Marylin so often. She didn't think his daddy would be happy to share."

"But Elio wasn't interested in fucking Marylin," King added in a low voice.

That was when it clicked, and I froze in place before turning to stare hard at Deviant, my hand drifting to the back of my pants and wrapping my fingers around the grip frame. "He figured Marylin could lead him to Britta."

The thought of what would have happened if he'd found her clouded my mind and made me want to feed someone bullets.

Deviant's eyes flickered to my arm, then returned to my face and narrowed. "Save it for Elio, Stone."

"Take your hand off your weapon," Fox ordered.

My hand clenched, and my trigger finger itched, but I did as I was told and released my gun before dropping my hand to my side.

Trying to contain my rage, I grunted, "When was this?"

"Two days ago."

"So we don't know if he went straight back to Marilyn in a tantrum and maybe even killed her?"

"We got lucky," Fox interrupted. "Francesco's inside man was given guard duty when Elio left town. As of this morning, Elio hasn't been to visit her again. He also said to tell you that Elio never physically harmed Marylin when he interrogated her. Tommaso had given the order that no one should touch her, and Elio was too afraid that someone would tattle on him to his daddy."

"Pussy," I spat, shaking my head.

"No argument," King agreed.

Fox's phone cut off anything that might have been said next, and he frowned when he saw the caller. "Grey," he told us before stabbing the screen to answer.

He listened for a second, then he cursed as his expression turned ruthless and deadly. "Thanks," he growled before hanging up and clenching the phone in a tight fist. "Tommaso is being released tomorrow. His lawyer supposedly found a piece of new evidence that got the case tossed."

"When?"

"First thing when the courthouse opens."

I glanced at the clock. "So we have just enough

time to get there but will only have a couple of hours to make a plan and set it in motion?"

Fox nodded, then began barking orders. "I'm gonna get on the line with Francesco, and we'll come up with some sort of plan." He looked directly at me. "I alerted Maverick, Whiskey, and several enforcers when you and Deviant came storming in here. They're armed and ready to ride. Get on the road with them, and we'll fill you in on your next moves when you get there."

I lifted my chin in acknowledgment and strode toward the door. As I left, I heard Fox tell King to get some of his enforcers and head to Chicago as well.

Before I could take off, I had to see Britta. She was still in my office, staring hard at her computer, but when she heard me enter, she jumped to her feet. "Any news?" she asked, wringing her hands together. "Did you find my mom?"

"Yeah. I'm sorry, baby, but I don't have time to give you more details. We have to leave immediately. I need you to promise me that you'll stay here. Remain in sight of one of my brothers unless you're locked in our room. I need to know you're safe, or I won't be able to concentrate on anything else."

"I promise," she whispered. "Now swear to me you'll come back in one piece."

My lips curved up, and I pulled her into my arms for a deep kiss. "I promise."

———

My brothers and I reached Chicago even faster than we'd expected, probably because we'd broken just about every speed limit along the way. Fox had sent me a message to meet the others at a warehouse not far from where Marylin was being held hostage.

When we arrived, a tall man with olive skin, dark hair, and shrewd green eyes approached me. He was clearly of Italian descent, so I assumed it was one of Francesco's men. "*Ciao*," he murmured, reaching out to shake my hand.

I was shocked when I immediately recognized his voice. "Francesco?"

I had expected him to send men, not be there himself.

"*Sì*. It's nice to finally meet you, but I would have preferred better circumstances."

"Agreed."

"Fox and I ran through many scenarios, but ultimately, we decided it was best to eliminate the threat altogether. We don't want to chance anyone finding loopholes and slithering their way out of the system."

I was relieved to hear that they wouldn't attempt to find another solution, like trying to fix it so that Tommaso and his key people ended up in jail. There would be no negotiation. Just a whole lot of pain before they ended up at the bottom of Lake Michigan.

"My sources tell me that Portia is currently at the office building with several other key players. When King arrives, he and his men will handle them. I have men on several warehouses waiting for the order to rescue anyone they find and take out whoever is holding them."

"That leaves Tommaso and Elio," I said, an evil smile curling my lips.

"Sì. We all agreed that it was your right to deal with them as you see fit."

I bobbed my head up and down in agreement.

"When Elio returned, Carlos was relieved of guard duty. However, before he left, he dropped subtle hints that it seemed like Marylin was ready to crack."

"Did he take the bait?"

"Sì." Francesco smiled, but it was sinister with a coldness in his eyes that would make most men cower. Coupled with his reputation for being merciless and extremely...creative with anyone who crossed him, it was easy to see why he was the head of the largest Mafia family in the Midwest.

"He is already waiting at the house, but the man I have watching it tells me that he hasn't gone past the front room. My assumption is that he's waiting for Tommaso, hoping his father will beat the truth out of Marylin."

"And Tommaso?"

"Currently being processed for release. We probably have about an hour before he arrives at the house."

"Thanks," I said as we shook hands again. "Couldn't have done this without you."

Francesco cocked his head and smirked. "My pleasure. You are aiding me in getting rid of a dirty organization. One that was trying to compete with me. We intend to send a very clear message about what happens to people who fuck with the Family."

I turned to head back to my bike but stopped when he spoke again. "Feel free to make Tommaso and Elio suffer as long as possible. After King takes care of the office building, he and his guys will be watching your backs at the house. When you're done, just leave everything behind. My cleaners will take care of it."

Damn, I seriously owed Francesco. And I had no doubt he'd eventually call in his chips.

When everyone had their orders, a few of our men left to help King while Maverick, Hunter, Racer, and I drove to a house a few streets over from our destination. Felicia and Donovan, a couple in Francesco's organization, lived there and hid our bikes in a shed in their backyard.

It would have been easier to wait for darkness, but after we'd been there about twenty minutes, Donovan came out back to tell us that Tommaso was ten minutes away.

Night made things easier, but it really didn't matter what time it was. We knew how to remain unnoticed. We split up across the street and took different routes to approach the house.

Deviant had provided the blueprints so we'd be familiar with the layout to avoid surprises. His best guess was that Marylin was either being held in the basement or the attic.

I crept up to the back door and glanced at Maverick. I was torn over saving my woman's mother and making the men responsible pay.

He narrowed his eyes and tapped my temple before whispering, "I'll get Marylin."

There was a bond between brothers, one that

was stronger than the ties of blood. And it meant that we knew each other in a way that outsiders never would. Maverick had known me for a long time, and after I patched, he'd seen the rage that lurked in my soul. It came out when we brought someone to The Room. I let it take over because punishing our enemies seemed to be the only time I had any peace. I couldn't take out the bastards who shot me and had killed so many people, including the hostage I was trying to save. But I could make others suffer in their stead.

Maverick knew what I hadn't wanted to admit. I had to be the one to deal with Tommaso and Elio, or the darkness inside me would fester and consume me. I was afraid that even Britta wouldn't be able to pull me back. Wiping out the threat to her would be the equivalent of saving those hostages and maybe it would douse the constant fury burning inside me.

The back door was the entrance to a small, dingy kitchen that clearly hadn't been cleaned in a very long time. If that was where they'd been feeding Marylin from, we'd be lucky if she wasn't sick. Maverick and Hunter split up, one going for a door that led to the basement and disappearing down the steps. The other paused at the door to a hallway where the stairs went up to the attic. The hallway was short and could be seen from most of the living room, so we had to wait for Elio to be distracted before Maverick could go for the stairs.

After what seemed like hours but was really only a few minutes, I heard creaking from the wooden board used to build the front porch. Elio walked over to open the door, and Maverick slipped up the stairs.

Racer and I drew our guns, holding them so that we were each trained on one of the men. When we heard the front door close, we moved through the hall into the living room.

"Hate to interrupt this little father and son reunion," Racer drawled, making both men whirl in our direction.

They went for their weapons but froze when I put a bullet in the ground right between Elio's legs. "I wouldn't do that, asshole. You wouldn't even be able to pull your gun before I blew your fucking head off."

"Sounds like fun," Racer said with a snicker. "Do you think they'd explode like pumpkins?"

I grinned, feeling a little of my wisecracking personality returning. "Watermelons," I quipped, making him chuckle. "But we'll have to test the theory another time. These two don't deserve a quick death."

"True."

Tommaso snorted in derision. "If your intent is to kill us, why are we just standing here?" He sounded bored, and my trigger finger twitched. "Waiting for someone else to come along and save your asses?"

"Nah," Maverick drawled from the doorway behind us. "These two are the most bloodthirsty out of all of us. They were just stalling so there was no risk to Marylin while we took her outta here."

Tommaso's face turned red and blotchy as he took a step forward. His hand swung toward his back, but he didn't get any farther before he screamed like a little girl, whipping his hand up to see a hole in his palm where my shot had gone straight through. "I warned you," I said with a shrug.

Elio sputtered curses but didn't make a move.

"Clear?" I asked Maverick.

"Yep. I'll be outside if you need anything. Oh, wait, the walls are soundproof...too bad we won't be able to hear their screams. Lucky Hunter, he brought a bag of toys for you."

I chuckled as I watched the color drain from Tommaso and Elio's faces.

Maverick's footsteps faded behind us as another set walked in, and a second later, Hunter dropped a duffel bag on the floor and plopped down onto the couch.

"Get rid of your weapons," I ordered.

Both men hesitated, and I cocked my gun, the sound seeming louder because of the dead silence in the room. Most guns didn't cock anymore, but I specifically carried one that did because I got a kick out of moments like this. The simple click could scare the piss out of some people.

Father and son emptied their holsters and pockets, tossing guns, knives, and other interesting items to Hunter. He put them in a bag and threw it into the fireplace. A specific instruction we'd been given from Francesco.

Several hours later, we took our toys into the kitchen to wipe off all the blood, leaving two mangled corpses behind.

"Let's get the fuck out of here," I grumbled. With Tommaso, Elio, and their associates out of the way, all I could think about was having Britta in my arms again.

We parted ways with King and his guys, then retrieved our bikes. Maverick met us at the apartment with an SUV. Our motorcycles would be transported home another way because we were driving with Marylin.

When we were an hour from Old Bridge, my cell beeped, and I looked to see that I'd received a text with links to several articles in the Chicago news. One about an accident in a high-rise in Chicago. Apparently, the carbon monoxide detectors had malfunctioned, and everyone on the top five floors had died from overexposure. Interestingly, no other floors seemed to be affected.

There was also a report of a house fire at an address belonging to P. Truitt. The fire investigators pinpointed the fireplace as the point of origin, saying that the occupants had clearly been careless, leaving loaded weapons near the flames that eventually exploded, burning the house to nothing but ashes.

I didn't bother to look for incidents at all the other locations we'd been involved in destroying.

The only thing I cared about was getting home to my woman.

11

BRITTA

Although Shaw had called to let me know that my mom was okay and he was bringing her to me, I needed to see her for myself. I paced back and forth in his room for the first couple of hours, then I headed downstairs and did the same in front of the bar. When I'd ridden down here with my mom two years ago, the drive had felt like it went so fast. But the three hours that I waited for them to pull into the compound felt as though it took forever.

Finally, Fox announced, "They just pulled through the gate."

I raced to the door, my gaze searching for my mom. Tears welled in my eyes when I saw Shaw help her out of an SUV. She must've been lying down because I hadn't seen her back there until he opened the door. As I ran toward them, I flashed him a grateful smile before throwing myself at my mom. "I'm so glad to see you. I was worried that we wouldn't find you in time."

"I'm okay, sweetie." She wrapped me up in a big hug. I had missed feeling her arms around me so much, all I could do was lean into her and cry.

After everything she had been through, I should've been the one to comfort her, but she seemed more pulled together than I was at the moment.

"We have so much to do to get our lives back." My mom scrubbed her hands down her face. "I'm sure our landlord has evicted us from the apartment in Chicago by now. It's been so long that he might have gotten rid of all of our stuff, too. We're probably going to need to bunk in a cheap motel for a little while, unless you want to go back to the place the Hounds of Hellfire got us instead. If we do that, maybe they'll let me keep my job. In Chicago, I'll have to start looking for a new one right away."

"Oh...um..." My gaze darted toward Shaw, and my mom's eyes narrowed.

"Who's that guy?" she asked. "He's been watching you the entire time we've been talking."

"Shaw," I whispered. "He's the Iron Rogues Captain here at the head chapter."

She quirked a brow. "And why is he looking at me like he'd gladly strangle me for talking about where we're going to live?"

"Because he's...um..." I struggled with finding the right word to describe our relationship without telling her that I loved him since I hadn't said the words to him yet. "Stone. My boyfriend."

It sounded almost ridiculous to use that word since he was so much more, but it was all I could come up with at that moment.

"You hooked up with Stone? The guy you've been thinking about for the past two years?"

Shaw closed the distance between us and slid his arm around me. "She did."

His answer didn't make my mom happy. Planting her fists on her hips, she huffed, "I might not know everything about MC life, but from what I understand, my daughter has not been claimed unless she's wearing your name on her back."

Shaw slid a loaded look at Fox, who headed down the hallway leading to Shaw's room. "Britta is very much mine."

"She's young and—"

Fox returned, holding a scrap of leather in his

hand that he tossed to Shaw, distracting my mom from whatever she'd been about to say.

Turning to me, Shaw showed me the back of the smaller version of his cut. I traced my fingers over the patch that said, "Property of Stone."

Happy tears streamed down my cheeks as he slid the leather vest onto my back. "How long have you had this?"

"Two long years."

His answer blew me away. "Really?"

He gripped the front of the vest and tugged me closer, his blue eyes filled with emotion as he confirmed, "It was the only comfort Fox could give me when he wouldn't share your location. I struggled hard with not knowing where you were. Knowing that I was going to make you my old lady as soon as we took care of the bastards who were after you and your mom was what allowed me to hold on for so long."

"That is...wow," I breathed.

"I almost gave it to you a dozen times, but it didn't feel right with what was going on with your mom," he explained. "I wanted to get you answers about her first."

"And you did better than that," I sniffed. "You brought her home to me."

There was a slight gleam of uncertainty in his eyes as he asked, "So this is home now?"

I nodded. "My home is with you, and you belong here. In Old Bridge. With the family you've built."

"Thank fuck because I wasn't looking forward to talking to Fox about me transferring to the chapter up in Chicago." He shook his head with a laugh. "I still hadn't come up with a plan for what to do if you and your mom decided that you wanted to head back to Hounds of Hellfire territory."

"Let me get this straight." Mom looked between the two of us. "You two barely interacted with each other the last time we were here but never forgot each other. Now you've been together for barely more than a week, and you're already his old lady?"

I beamed a smile at her. "Yeah, that's exactly right."

"Actually, it's not," Shaw corrected. I turned toward him, my eyes widening when he pulled a diamond solitaire out of his pocket. Sliding the ring onto my finger, he added, "She's not just my old lady. She's the woman I'm going to marry as soon as I can get her down the aisle."

"Oh my gosh." I blinked down at the sparkling gemstone, even more stunned than I'd been when

Shaw had shown me the property patch. "How about tomorrow?"

I meant it as a joke, but Shaw took me seriously. "I'm sure Molly and Dahlia can get a wedding organized for us that quickly with the help of the other old ladies."

"I was being held hostage only four hours ago," my mom grumbled. "There is no chance I'll be ready to walk my baby down the aisle to you by tomorrow."

"Take a little more time, but not too much," Shaw offered. "I'm not gonna wait long to make the woman I love my wife."

"Love?" I echoed, pressing trembling fingers to my lips.

"I can't fucking believe I forgot to give you those three little words while I proposed." He brushed his lips against mine. "It didn't go how I planned, but I was thrown off by the possibility that your mom was gonna convince you to leave with her."

"That was never going to happen, Shaw." I stroked my palms up his chest before twining my arms around his neck. "I love you too much to ever leave you."

"Thank fuck," he rasped, claiming my mouth in a deep kiss that had everyone from the Iron Rogues cheering while my mom shook her head with a laugh. "Because I love you so damn much, baby."

EPILOGUE

BRITTA

It was amazing the difference one year had made in my life. My mom was healthy and happily single. We lived in Tennessee now. And I was pregnant with my husband's baby—due any day now, in fact.

One thing hadn't changed, though. I didn't expect anything special for my birthday. Except maybe to give birth to our baby girl. But I hadn't felt a single twinge all day. Not even having lots of sex with Shaw this morning had helped.

"What's that pout for, baby?" Shaw tugged at the bottom lip I had puffed out. "Are you not feeling up to going out for dinner?"

The orgasms he had given me this morning weren't the only present I had gotten today.

Although Shaw hadn't gone totally overboard, he had made me breakfast in bed. That, along with a pretty bouquet and the diamond pendant that matched my engagement ring had made today the best birthday I'd ever had.

"Nope, I'm good." I patted my rounded belly. "Maybe if I eat something super spicy, I'll finally go into labor."

"I never should've let you read my pregnancy books," he muttered.

Shaw had bought just about every book on the market when we found out that I was carrying his baby. I'd wanted to light them on fire because what he read had only made him even more overprotective, but when I got frustrated over not being dilated at all during my doctor's appointment a few days ago, I checked each one of them for advice on how to induce labor naturally.

Nothing helped. Not the red raspberry leaf tea I drank last night, or the nipple stimulation and sex. "Our daughter is proving to be as stubborn as her daddy."

"She'll come out when she's ready."

Since that was what he always said when I complained, I just shook my head with a sigh. Glancing out the window of the SUV he bought the day after my positive pregnancy test, I drew my brows together. "I thought we were going to my favorite Mexican restaurant?"

"Just gotta stop at the clubhouse for a minute. We'll be in and out in a jiffy."

I didn't question his explanation because it wasn't unusual for him to need to pick up paperwork from his office there after we moved into our house. There were several motorcycles parked in front of the clubhouse when we pulled up, but that was normal too.

Shaw must have counted on me needing to pee to get me inside—which was a safe assumption since our baby girl liked to bounce on my bladder. When we walked in the door, the entire front area was full of friends and family, who all yelled, "Surprise!"

"Oh my gosh," I squealed, stunned to see the place decorated with streamers and balloons. "Is this all for me?"

"Damn straight." Shaw gave me a quick kiss before beaming a smile at me. "I couldn't let my wife's birthday pass by without doing something extra special."

"Thank you," I gasped before my mom rushed over to give me a hug.

"Anything to make you happy, baby," he

murmured in the rush of people who followed her, staying by my side.

"I can't believe Izzy is here too," I cried after everyone finished greeting us. The last time I saw her was on my wedding day, but we talked on the phone all the time now that the danger to my mom and me had passed. "How did you pull all of this off without me knowing?"

"I had a lot of help. Wasn't sure about throwing you a surprise party with you being so close to your due date, but all the old ladies told me that I was being ridiculous," he murmured, pulling me against his side.

Tilting my head back to smile at him, I asked, "Did they actually say ridiculous?"

"Only your mom." He shook his head with a laugh. "The other old ladies said some shit along the lines of me being an overprotective, macho, alpha male."

Picturing how that conversation went down, I giggled. "They'd know since they're all married to their own Neanderthals."

My mom joined us, wagging her brows. "Maybe it's time I found one of my own."

"It's not like I can stop you from dating." I wagged my finger at her. "But Shaw is going to look into any guy who you go out with. If he says they're no good, then you don't go."

She rolled her eyes. "I think you forgot that I'm the mom and you're the daughter."

I loved my mom, and she had been so helpful during my pregnancy, but that didn't mean I would ever trust her taste in men. "Yeah, well...I'm going to be a mom too any day now, and I want my daughter to have her grandmother in her life, happy and healthy."

"And no way in hell am I letting anybody I don't trust near my wife and child," Shaw growled.

She held her hands up in a gesture of surrender. "Okay. Fine, my son-in-law can do background checks on as many guys as he wants, just so long as I get plenty of time with my granddaughter so I can spoil her properly."

A sharp pain rolled over my stomach, and I almost doubled over. "We got that figured out in the nick of time. We need to go to the hospital now."

Danica had taken her sweet time, going a week past my due date. But she hurried up once she was ready to be born, only taking three hours after we got to the hospital.

EPILOGUE

STONE

When I left our house this morning, Britta had been practically drooling at the sight of me. She loved when I was dressed in a tailored suit —even admitted once that it was because I radiated power and determination. Which turned her the fuck on...something that I didn't hesitate to take advantage of.

There was a moment before I walked out the door when I thought she was going to jump me. If I didn't have to be at the courthouse on time, I would've given her more time to consider it, but we'd already used up all of the extra hour I'd given myself when she joined me in the shower earlier.

It wasn't often that I had to go to court. The last time, she'd been pregnant, so I had insisted that she stay home. This was her first real chance to see me in action, so I wasn't surprised to see her slip inside the courtroom shortly before I gave my opening statement.

I needed to focus on the case since one of my brothers was depending on me, but it was hard as fuck to concentrate when each time I glanced at Britta, she wiggled in her seat as though her panties were about to disintegrate.

Walking back to the defendant's table after questioning a witness, I couldn't help but flash her a cocky smirk and a wink. The look she sent my way made me regret that since my suit pants didn't do a great job hiding my hard-on. Tugging on my collar and shifting in my seat to find a more comfortable position, I took a few deep breaths to try to cool myself off.

It didn't work. Before I had to get up again and give everyone a good look at what belonged only to Britta, I asked the judge for a recess. Thank fuck that the judge agreed to my request.

I didn't waste a second darting out of the courtroom.

Britta wasn't in sight, so I called her phone, and she picked up immediately.

"Where the fuck are you?" I growled.

Her voice was breathless when she replied, making my dick swell even more. "Outside on the steps."

"Get your pretty little ass back in here."

I knew it would only take a couple of minutes, but I was impatient, so I paced while I waited and practically growled at anyone who got too close.

When I spotted my wife, I stalked over and grabbed her hand, then tugged her behind me down a hallway. We were moving fast, but I was conscious of how much longer my legs were than hers, so I made sure she didn't trip.

The hallway was busy, but everyone was so focused on their own thoughts that they didn't seem to notice us.

Finally, I saw the door I was looking for and stopped in front of it. Whipping out a key, I unlocked it and shoved it open, pulling her inside. Then I slammed the door shut behind us. After flicking the lock, I backed her up against the door and caged her in with my hands on both sides of her.

"Did you wear this sexy little dress to tease me, Britta?" I grunted. My hands dropped to the hem and slipped underneath to glide up her silky thighs.

"Maybe," she teased. "Why aren't you in court?"

I blew out a breath, then dropped my head and

kissed the damp skin of her neck. I kept working my way down, muffling my answer. "Couldn't wait another fucking second to be inside you. Asked for a recess, and thank fuck, the judge agreed."

"Nice."

I knew it gave her a little feminine thrill that she had that effect on me. "Feeling a little smug about that, baby?"

She giggled, but it morphed into a moan when I curled my fingers into the waistband of her panties. "It's only fair. You looked like sex in a suit," she breathed. "It was making me want you so bad."

I yanked her underwear and ripped it away, then brought the lacy material to my nose and inhaled deeply before shoving them in my pocket. "I love that you get so fucking wet for me."

I didn't have much time, but I wouldn't have been able to hold back anyway. So I used one hand to pull down the top of her dress while the other plundered her drenched pussy.

Each breast popped out when I lowered the cup of her bra, and I sucked on her nipples until she was writhing in desperation.

"I want to taste you so fucking much, baby, but we've gotta be quick."

Withdrawing my hand from between her legs, I

licked my fingers clean and groaned. "That'll have to do for now, but I'm warning you now, I'm gonna spend all night with my mouth on your delicious pussy."

I knew talking dirty revved her up, so I grinned when she shuddered and moaned, her hands clenched in my hair.

Putting my hands under her ass, I lifted her and walked over to one of the chairs surrounding a large table in the conference room. I kicked it out with my foot and sat down, positioning Britta to straddle me.

"Take me out," I ordered.

I played with her gorgeous tits while she unbuckled my belt, then lowered my zipper and wrapped her hand as far as it would go around my cock.

She cried out when I twisted and plucked her tight buds, and I stopped moving, giving her a look of warning. "You have to be quiet, Britta. No one gets to hear you in the throes of ecstasy but me. Is that clear?"

She nodded frantically.

"If you can't be quiet, I'll stop."

"I can," she whispered. "I'll stay quiet."

"Such a good girl," I murmured.

I moved her hand away from my dick and put her

arms around my neck. Then I raised her hips and lined her pussy up with my shaft. When I jerked her down, impaling her completely, she dropped her head back but bit her lip to keep from making a sound.

"Ride my cock, baby," I commanded in a low, raspy voice.

I kept my hands on her hips to help her bounce on my dick but let her be in charge.

"Fuck," I rasped as her inner muscles gripped me tight, fighting to keep me inside as she raised off my cock. "Your pussy can't get enough, can it? Fuck, baby, that's it. Don't let me go. Oh, fuck yeah."

She bore down even more, and I groaned as I took over, moving her up and down and bucking my hips to meet her.

"Shaw," she whispered in a ragged voice. "Oh, yes. I need it harder."

I moved my knees apart, forcing her legs to open even wider as I upped my pace and intensity, slamming up as I yanked her down. I was so deep, I bumped her cervix every time I filled her.

"So fucking hot," I grunted. "Love being inside you. That's it. Ride me hard, baby. Oh, fuck! Fuck, Britta! Yes! Fuck!"

I knew I was getting louder, but I couldn't seem

to control it. Britta grabbed my face and sealed our mouths together, swallowing my sounds and driving me wild with her seductive tongue.

After a few minutes, I tore my mouth from hers and put my lips next to her ear. "Do you feel how deep I am, baby? Remember what it felt like when I stuffed you so full of come that it was dripping down your thighs? I fucked you so deep, I left my baby in you."

Britta moaned, and I bit her earlobe before speaking again. "Do you want me to put another baby inside you? 'Cause I'm dying to see you round and swollen again. I miss seeing proof that I bred you while I take your tight pussy. Sucking on your milky tits. Do you want that?"

"Yes!" she shouted.

I was beyond stopping, so I slapped a hand over her mouth and fucked her hard and fast until she was screaming into my palm. Then I planted myself as deep as possible and let go, releasing spurt after spurt of hot come into her womb.

I got what I wanted. Nine months later, we had a healthy baby boy.

But that wasn't the only time a suit and an opening statement got her knocked up.

Curious about the Hounds of Hellfire? They were introduced in Mac!

Wonder what's up with Nic DeLuca? His story is The Mafia Boss's Nanny!

And if you join our newsletter, you'll get an email from us with a link to claim a FREE copy of The Virgin's Guardian, which was banned on Amazon.

ABOUT THE AUTHOR

The writing duo of Elle Christensen and Rochelle Paige team up under the Fiona Davenport pen name to bring you sexy, insta-love stories filled with alpha males. If you want a quick & dirty read with a guaranteed happily ever after, then give Fiona Davenport a try!

Printed in Great Britain
by Amazon